Jim Henson's
BIG BOOK OF
MUPPET™
STORIES

Jim Henson's
─ BIG BOOK OF ─
MUPPET™
STORIES

DERRYDALE

THIS IS A CARLTON BOOK

This 1994 edition published by Derrydale Books,
distributed by Outlet Book Company, Inc.,
a Random House Company,
40 Engelhard Avenue, Avenel, New Jersey 07001.

Random House
New York • Toronto • London • Sydney • Auckland

ISBN 0-517-10229-3

Printed in Spain.

Contents

Fozzie's Not Invited

"Bzzzz, bzzzzz, picnic, bzzz, bzzzz, fun."

Those were the words that drifted on the breeze toward Fozzie as he passed by Kermit's front porch one warm spring morning. Fozzie could see Gonzo and Kermit sitting close together on the porch, laughing and talking.

By Ellen Weiss   *Illustrated by Richard Walz*

Fozzie waved as he walked past.

"Hmmm," he said to himself, "Sounds as though maybe there's going to be a picnic. This is great weather for it. I wonder why nobody told me about it."

Farther down the street, Fozzie saw Piggy and Janice saying good-bye to Rowlf in front of the supermarket.

"See you at the picnic!" called Piggy as Rowlf went into the store.

"Hmmmm," said Fozzie to himself. "It seems as if everybody knows about this picnic but me."

As it happened, Fozzie was also on his way to the supermarket. He looked for Rowlf when he got inside, but didn't bump into him until they were in the checkout line

"Hi, there," said Rowlf, smiling.

Fozzie couldn't help looking to see what was in Rowlf's shopping cart. There were rolls, carrot sticks, bananas and oranges, peanut butter and jelly, paper plates, napkins, and juice. Picnic stuff, it looked like to Fozzie.

"So, ah, Rowlf,"saidFozzie carefully. "Doing some, er, picnic shopping?"

"Sure am," said Rowlf. "It's going to be a great afternoon."

"Gee," said Fozzie.

"That's terrific."

Could it really be? Were all his friends having a picnic and not inviting him? It was too awful to think about. Fozzie decided not to think about it. Maybe, he hoped, just maybe he'd made some mistake.

His next stop was the drugstore, to buy some toothpaste. Right in the middle of the toothpaste aisle, who should he run into but Piggy, Animal, and Janice.

"Hi," said Fozzie. "Picking up a few things?"

"Fer sure," said Janice." We're buying picnic stuff." She held up a can of bug spray and a bottle of suntan lotion.

"Picnic! Picnic!" yelled Animal.

So it was true. They were all having a picnic, and they weren't inviting him. How could this be happening? He had thought they were all such good friends. Were they mad at him? Had he done something to hurt them? Or, were there lots of things he didn't get invited to?

Fozzie had never felt so hurt in his life.

He walked and walked, hardly seeing what was around him. Finally, his feet took him to the bus station at the edge of town.

And there, sitting on a bench were Kermit, Gonzo, Piggy, Janice, Animal, and Rowlf. They had two big picnic baskets and a large, red checked tablecloth.

"Fozzie!" cried Kermit "Where have you been, anyway? We thought we were going to miss the bus, waiting for you!"

"Waiting for me?" echoed Fozzie in confusion. "Why were you waiting for me?"

"To go to the picnic, silly," said Piggy.

"But—but you didn't invite me!" said Fozzie.

"Of course we did," said Kermit. "Piggy did." Kermit turned to Piggy. "Didn't you?" he said.

"I thought you said you were going to ask him," she said.

"No, I thought you were going to!" said Kermit.

"And I thought Janice was going to," said Rowlf.

They all looked sheepish.

"I guess we messed up," said Kermit. "We certainly meant to ask you. We would never leave you out on purpose. We're friends!"

Fozzie beamed happily.

"Say, Fozzie," said Rowlf, "how come you didn't say anything to me before when we were talking about the picnic?"

"I was feeling too hurt to ask," said Fozzie. "I guess, if I ever feel left out again, I should say something about it."

"I sure hope you do," said Kermit as the bus pulled up. "But I sure hope it doesn't happen again."

The driver opened the bus door.

"Where to?" he asked them.

"To the country," said Fozzie happily. "My friends and I are going to have a picnic!"

Far-Out Talent

It was almost show time at the Muppet Theater. The singing chickens were warming up, the juggling hippos were practicing, and Fozzie Bear was trying out his new jokes.

"Kermit! Kermit! Hold everything!" Scooter came running in, looking very excited.

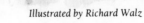

By Richard Chevat   *Illustrated by Richard Walz*

"What's wrong?" Kermit asked impatiently. "Did the penguins forget their bow ties again?"

"No, no!" Scooter cried. "Creatures from outer space have landed!"

"Creatures from outer space!" Kermit said nervously. "Are they here to invade earth?"

"I don't think so," said Scooter. "They look pretty friendly."

Everyone gathered around as a group of six strange-looking space creatures appeared backstage.

No one had ever seen anything like them. They each had three arms, five green eyes, and bright orange fur. But strangest of all were the small propellers on the tops of their heads.

One of the space creatures stepped forward. The propeller on his head started to spin, and soon he was floating a few inches off the floor.

"Hello, green creature," the floating space visitor said to Kermit.

"Kermit!" said Gonzo excitedly. "They're great! Maybe we could put them in the show!"

Kermit thought for a few seconds.

"Gee, I don't know," he said, turning to the aliens. "Do you guys have an act?"

"What is an ax?" the creature asked in its weird voice.

11

"You know," explained Kermit, "something to do onstage. Do you dance?"

"Dunce? What is dunce?" asked the space being as he slowly flew around Kermit.

"Hey, I have an idea!" Gonzo said. "You can sing with the singing chickens!"

"Zing? We no zing," all the aliens said sadly. Then **they too** rose up into the air.

"Maybe they play music," suggested Rowlf.

"No musics," they replied, while they floated around the room.

"How about telling jokes?" said Fozzie. "Did you hear the one about the two Martians? They wanted to stay overnight on the moon, but they couldn't because the moon was full. Get it? A full moon! Wocka, wocka!"

"Hmmm, jukes. No, we know no jukes," said the first creature.

He was so sad that his teeth almost touched the ground.

"I'm sorry," said Kermit. "But you don't dance, sing, play music, or tell jokes. I just don't know what you could do in the show."

"We no have ax," the alien agreed. "We go home."

And slowly they flew out the door.

"Gee, too bad," said Gonzo. "They seemed like nice space creatures."

"Yeah," Fozzie nodded. "I wish they did something besides fly around all the time."

"Yeah," added Kermit. "'They sure did fly a lot."

Then suddenly he had an idea.

"Hey! They can fly! That would be a great act! Scooter, go catch them, quick!"

Soon the space creatures were onstage, flying around and doing flips and rolls in the air.

The audience cheered and applauded.

"You guys can perform here every night," Kermit said to them after the show.

"No, thanks," said the aliens' leader. "We must go now."

"But why?" asked Kermit.

"You were great!"

"No can stay," explained the creature as he floated to the door. "Must return to our planet with valuable discovery—jukes! Did you hear the one about the two Martians?"

"Good-bye!" everyone shouted as the spaceship took off and flew away.

"Come back soon!" called Kermit. We really loved your ax!"

The Garage Sale

Every spring, Miss Piggy cleaned up her house from top to bottom. Every spring, she washed windows, aired out pillows, and beat rugs. And every spring, she noticed that she had more and more things to clean.

One year, it just got to be too much.

By Harry Ross

Illustrated by Richard Walz

14

"This house is too crowded," she said to herself. "I think I'll throw out some of this old junk I never use."

She was just about to get out the jumbo garbage bags when she had an idea.

"I'll have a garage sale!" she said.

She went to the store and got some tagboard and a hot pink marker and made a sign. It said:

COME ONE! COME ALL!
GARAGE SALE TOMORROW!
GREAT STUFF!

She posted the sign on her front lawn and then gathered together the things she wanted to get rid of.

There was her pink bowling ball from the Piggyback League.
There were her sugarplum fairy wings from the costume ball.
There were some ski boots that rubbed and some sandals that squeaked and an old kitty cat clock that went *tock tick* instead of *tick tock*.
There was a box of old books and beauty magazines.

Bright and early the next day, she brought everything out to her garage.

Kermit was the first to come. "Interesting clock," he said.

Piggy looked at the kitty cat clock and remembered the Christmas morning she had found it beneath her tree. It *was* cute.

"It says *tock tick* instead of *tick tock*," she pointed out.

"I still like it," said Kermit.

"So do I," said Piggy. "I'm sorry, Kermie, I've changed my mind. It's not for sale."

"Okay," said Kermit. He moved on to look at something else.

Then Gonzo showed up.

"Hey, these wings are really nifty," he said, trying them on.

When she saw them on Gonzo, Piggy remembered the costume ball and how ravishing she had looked.

"They *are* nifty," she agreed. "I'm sorry, Gonzo. They're not for sale. Besides, they don't do a thing for you."

Fozzie was fiddling with the boots, Rowlf was rummaging through the old books, and Animal was trying to jam the squeaky sandals onto his feet.

Suddenly, Piggy could not stand it for one more second.

"Hold everything!" she yelled, so loudly that Kermit dropped the bowling ball half an inch from his toe.

"I've changed my mind," continued Piggy in a very small voice. "I'm sorry, but the garage sale is off."

Everyone stood still, amazed.

"Just because I don't use these things anymore," explained Piggy, "it doesn't mean I don't need them. They bring back wonderful memories. Each one of these is a part of me. These things are really special to me . . . and I want to keep them. Please forgive me, everyone."

"We understand," said Kermit, smiling.

"Sure we do," said Gonzo. "But there is one thing I'd still really like to buy."

"Gonzo, whatever it is, it's not for sale," said Piggy in exasperation.

"I'll bet it is," said Gonzo. "I really want to buy that nice garage sale sign, Piggy. You see, I have a lot of great stuff I don't need anymore, and—"

"No, Gonzo," laughed Piggy. "It's still not for sale." She began gathering up her beloved things to take inside. "It's free. You can have it!"

Hike on Dragon Mountain

Dragon Mountain was the biggest mountain around. Its
western slope was shaped like a dragon's head and was covered
with jagged trees that looked just like long, snaggly teeth.

Climbing the steep slopes of Dragon Mountain was hard work,
and it was scary, too. But year after year, the bravest Frog Scouts
made the trip, hoping to earn their mountaineering badges.

By Deborah Kovacs   *Illustrated by Richard Walz*

One day, Robin came running up to Kermit.

"Uncle Kermit!" he shouted. "I'm going to climb Dragon Mountain today. Do you want to go with me?

"Good old Dragon Mountain," said Kermit. "Why, I haven't climbed it since I was a Frog Scout myself. Let's go!"

In an hour, Robin and Kermit were on the trail.

"What a great day," said Robin.

And it was. The sun was shining, and the sky was blue.

After a little while, they got to the part of the mountain called Dragon's Neck. Here, the trail went straight up.

"Sheesh! This mountain is a lot steeper than when I was a Frog Scout!" said Kermit, puffing and wheezing.

He stopped to rest and suddenly noticed that Robin was no longer behind him.

"Robin?" he called. "Robin?"

"Coming, Uncle Kermit," said Robin, scurrying up from behind.

"What happened to you?" said Kermit.

"I was just following these 'Frog Scout Rules for Safe Mountain Hiking,'" said Robin, holding up a little book.

"Okay," said Kermit. "But stay with me from now on."

They climbed, and they climbed, and at last they reached the highest point of Dragon Mountain. It was a pointy peak with a twisted pine tree on top of it. They could see far into the distance in every direction. The air was clear and sweet. The only sound they heard was the whistling of the wind in the trees.

"What a great day to climb a mountain," said Robin. "I can't wait to watch the sunset," he added, pointing to the reddening western sky.

"SUNSET?" said Kermit. "We'd better get going, or we'll get lost in the dark!"

Quickly they started down the mountain.

For a while, the scurried along the shadowy trail in silence. Then they came to a place were it branched off in many directions.

"Let's see . . . " said Kermit, trying to figure out which way to go. "Oh, yes! I remember this big rock here," he added, slapping a large gray boulder with confidence. "We'll take a right turn here." He turned right and stopped.

"Uncle Kermit?" said Robin.

"Wait a second, I'm thinking," said Kermit. "This doesn't look right. Let's try going this way."

He started off in another direction.

"No, it's over this way," he said. Then he stopped suddenly and looked around in the growing gloom. He blinked his eyes.

Something didn't feel right.

"Uncle Kermit?" said Robin.

"Not now, Robin," said Kermit. "I have to think."

Through the woods, a low, howling sound began.

"Wh-wh-what's that?" Kermit said.

"Oh, that's the call of the night-singing shrike," said Robin. "We learned all about birdcalls at Frog Scouts."

"Sounds more like a night-singing shriek to me," muttered Kermit under his breath. "It's definitely time to go home."

"Uncle Kermit? Why don't we just look for the white rags that I tied to the trees as we hiked up?" Robin pointed to the one right next to him on the trail.

"Amazing!" said Kermit. "That was a great idea!"

Robin held up his Frog Scout book. "It was right here, on page twelve," he said.

"What a scout!" said Kermit. "I've really forgotten a lot since I was a Frog Scout. It's a good thing I'm with you!"

"Shucks, it was nothing," said Robin.

And with the rags gleaming in the darkening sky, they easily found their way back down the mountain.

"You did it!" said Kermit. "Now you'll get your badge."

"No, we did it, Uncle Kermit. And I'm going to keep my new mountaineering badge right next to your old one," said Robin, smiling proudly.

Up, Up, and Away

On the day the big fair came to town, Gonzo was so excited he could hardly wait for the gates to open.

By Louise Gikow

Illustrated by Richard Walz

He was the first one into the fairgrounds, the first one to ride on the Ferris wheel, and the first one to see the great big sign with the fancy blue letters.

"OWNER OF HOT-AIR BALLOON NEEDS SENSIBLE, RELIABLE ASSISTANT," it said. "SEE MR. SAMMIS."

"What a great job!" thought Gonzo. "I love hot-air balloons."

He immediately ran off to find Mr. Sammis and ask him for the job.

Mr. Sammis looked carefully at Gonzo. "Taking care of my balloon is hard work," he said. "All kinds of things could go wrong. Are you sensible and reliable?"

"Absolutely!" said Gonzo. "I'm sensible from head to toe, and I'm as reliable as the day is long. Please give me a chance."

"Well, I'll try you out," said Mr. Sammis. "Watch the balloon while I go to the store. Don't let anyone touch it."

"Yippee!" said Gonzo.

He sat down next to the balloon and tried to look reliable.

A kitten walked by.

"Hello, kitty!" said Gonzo.

The kitten glanced at Gonzo, and then it hopped into the balloon's wicker basket.

"No, kitty!" cried Gonzo, leaping up. "'You're not allowed to go in there!"

But the kitten just looked at Gonzo, looked down at the ground below, and then mewed as if its heart would break.

"That cat can't get down!" Gonzo realized. "But no one is supposed to touch the balloon, not even me! I need to use good sense. But what's the sensible thing to do?"

The kitten mewed again.

"I have to save that cat!" decided Gonzo.

He climbed into the balloon's basket. But on the way, he accidentally knocked aside the ropes that held the balloon to the ground. The balloon began to climb into the air. Soon the ground was far away, and the balloon was skimming along, bumping the tops of trees.

Gonzo could see Mr. Sammis returning.

"HELP!!!" Gonzo called.

Mr. Sammis began running along on the ground, following the balloon.

"Turn the red knob to the left!" he cried.

Gonzo searched for the red knob.

"I can't find it!" he yelled.

The balloon wafted past the Ferris wheel, much too close for comfort.

"On your right! On your right! Turn the knob!" called Mr. Sammis.

Finally, Gonzo found the knob and turned it.

Gradually, the balloon began to lower, and at last it came to rest in a field just outside the fairgrounds.

Mr. Sammis quickly tied it down, and then he turned to Gonzo. "What happened?" he asked.

Miserably, Gonzo held up the kitten, who was now purring loudly.

"Ariel!" said Mr. Sammis.

"My cat! Did she jump into the basket?"

"Yes!" said Gonzo. "She looked so scared, I had to save her. But somehow I kicked the ropes off by mistake. Now you'll never believe that I'm sensible and reliable," he finished sadly.

"Yes, I will, Gonzo," said Mr. Sammis kindly. "I believe you're sensible enough to help an animal you think is in trouble. And I know I can rely on you to tell the truth. I just need to give you easier things to do to begin with."

He patted Gonzo on the back. "Now, how about a little ride?"

"I think I'm going to like this job!" said Gonzo happily, as they floated up into the sky.

The Sky's the Limit

Sometimes when they aren't busy, Gonzo, Mr. Sammis, and Ariel take trips in their hot-air balloon. Would you like to go with them this time? Just climb aboard! Wow! The higher up you go, the smaller things look down below. The trees seem tiny enough to scoop up and put into your pocket. The pond looks little enough to drink in one big gulp. And all the people on the ground look as if you could hold them in the palm of your hand! On these high-flying adventures, Gonzo likes to look down below and count the things he sees. Count them with him. See if you can find:

1 boat   **2 cars**   **3 cows**

4 people   **5 houses**

Fozzie's New Partner

"Oh, woe is me," said Fozzie Bear as he walked away from the big stage. Fozzie had just finished performing in his smash hit, one-bear show—"The Funniest Bear Anywhere."

"But, Fozzie, the audience loved you," said Kermit. "What could be wrong?"

By Jim Lewis

Illustrated by Richard Walz

"Sigh!" sighed Fozzie. "The audience only laughed at most of my jokes. I want people to laugh at everything I say."

"Everything?" mused Kermit. "Hmm, if you're sure that's what you want, I know who can help you."

"You do?" asked Fozzie, who was now feeling very excited.

"Go to Muppet Labs and see Dr. Bunsen Honeydew and Beaker," said Kermit, and before he could say good-bye, Fozzie was gone.

"Knock-knock!" called Fozzie when he came to the door of Muppet Labs.

"Who's there?" asked Dr. Honeydew.

"Canoe."

"Canoe who?"

"Canoe help me find someone who will laugh at everything I say?" said Fozzie.

"Of course we can, Mr. Bear," said Dr. Honeydew. "At Muppet Labs our motto is: 'Nothing Is Impossible, Although Many Things Are Extremely Messy.' Please allow me to introduce Loopy, the world's first laughing robot!"

Dr. Honeydew pressed a button, and with a "WHIRRRRRR!" a "BLEEEEEP!" and a "BLINKITY-BLONKITY-BLOOP!" out rolled Loopy.

"Good luck, Mr. Bear," said Dr. Honeydew. "We must return to our experiment. We're trying to find a cure for brussels sprouts."

Fozzie was overjoyed, excited, and generally very happy, too.

"C'mon, Loopy!" he called. "Now I'll have an audience that laughs at everything I say!"

Right away, Loopy began to laugh. He had a great big robot laugh that sounded like this:

"HAWAH-HAWAH-HAWAH-HAWAH-HAWAH!"

"Wait! That's not the joke," said Fozzie.

And Loopy laughed even harder: "HAWAH-HAWAH-HAWAH-HAWAH-HAWAH-HAWAH!"

"Loopy! You're not supposed to laugh yet!" said Fozzie.

But by now Loopy was laughing so hard that Fozzie had to shout.

This, of course, made Loopy laugh louder still. "HAWAH-HAWAH-HAWAH-HAWAH-HAWAH-HAWAH!"

Fozzie ran back to Muppet Labs, where Dr. Honeydew was watching Beaker juggle brussels sprouts.

"You've got to help me!" called Fozzie. "Loopy won't stop laughing!"

"But, Mr. Bear," said Dr. Honeydew. "You wanted someone who would laugh at everything you say."

"Gosh," said Fozzie. "If someone is always laughing, then you never know which jokes are really funny."

"An excellent deduction, Mr. Bear," said Dr. Honeydew, hitting the Muppet Labs robot recall button.

Loopy rolled back into the lab with a "WHIRRRRR!" and a "BLEEEEEP!" a "BLINKITY-BLONKITY-BLOOOP!" and, of course, "HAWAH-HAWAH-HAWAH-HAWAH-HAWAH!"

"Thanks, Dr. Honeydew," said Fozzie.

"Memememe!" squeaked Beaker.

"That's right," chuckled Dr. Honeydew. "Who would have thought Fozzie would find the sound of laughter un*bear*able! Heh-heh."

"Wocka! Wocka!" said Fozzie.

Piggy's New Leaf

Miss Piggy looked around her kitchen and sighed.
Kermit, Fozzie, and Gonzo had come for lunch, and the room
was a mess.

By Louise Gikow

Illustrated by Richard Walz

Fozzie had shown everyone his new juggling act, and now there were peas stuck to the ceiling.

Gonzo had dripped mashed poatoes all over the table.

And there were dirty dishes everywhere.

Piggy had begun to pick up the dishes when she noticed something on the floor. She bent down to pick it up. It was a book.

Then she remembered. Fozzie had given this very book to Kermit for his birthday. Kermit had been talking about it for days. He was really enjoying it.

"Hmmmm," thought Piggy. "I wonder if it's good."

She sat down, just for a moment, opened the book to page one, and began to read.

It was a wonderful book, and she read on and on.

She forgot all about doing the dishes or cleaning up the kitchen.

As she continued reading, her elbow inched closer and closer to a half-empty glass of chocolate milk on the table. And when she lifted her arm to turn the page—oh, no! The glass tilted, and the chocolate milk spilled all over Kermit's new book!

Piggy grabbed for a napkin and tried to wipe up the mess, but it was no use. The book was soggy and ruined. And just at that moment, Kermit walked in the back door.

"Piggy?" he asked. "Did I leave my book here?"

"Uh . . . uh . . . no, I don't think so, Kermie," sputtered Piggy, hiding the book behind her back. "I've been cleaning, and I didn't see it."

"Gee," said Kermit. "It seems to be missing. I guess I'll go home and look some more."

When Kermit had gone, Piggy wrapped the book in a dish towel. Then she rushed up to her room and hid the book under her bed.

Kermit spent the next few days looking for the book. Of course, he didn't find it. And Piggy felt worse and worse.

"If Kermit ever finds out what happened," she worried, "he'll never speak to me again. What am I going to do?"

But then she came up with a plan. All she had to do was to buy a new book for Kermit and pretend she had found it. He would never know.

So Piggy sneaked out to the bookstore. She found the book on the shelf.

But when she went to the cash register to pay for it, who should she find there but Kermit himself—with another copy of the book in his hands.

"Gee, Piggy," said Kermit. "This is really nice of you. But I should buy the book myself. After all, I lost it."

"No, you didn't!" Piggy blurted out. "Oh, Kermie, it was all my fault. I was reading your book, and the chocolate milk spilled on it, and I hid it because I was afraid you'd never talk to me again, and now you probably hate me!"

And Miss Piggy burst into tears.

"Piggy," Kermit said gently. "You're my friend. I don't hate you. But it would have been easier if you had told me right away."

"You're right," sniffed Piggy. "I'll never do anything like this again."

And she never did.

Kermit and the Best Present of All

It was Saturday night, and Kermit was rushing around his house plumping pillows and straightening pictures. He only had a few minutes before all his guests arrived. Everything had to be just right for Fozzie's surprise party.

By Marianne Meyer

Illustrated by Richard Walz

There would be games, balloons, cake, and a big "Happy Birthday" banner that Kermit had made from an old blanket.

At last, the doorbell rang. Kermit ran to answer it and found all his friends standing in the hall.

"Hi, everybody!" he called to his guests. "C'mon in!"

Rowlf entered first, carrying a package wrapped in pretty paper with musical notes on it.

"Where do we put the presents?" he asked cheerfully.

"Presents?" gasped Kermit. "Yikes! I was so busy blowing up balloons, baking the cake, mixing up the punch, and doing everything else, I totally forgot a present for Fozzie! Now what'll I do?"

"Couldn't you wrap up something in the house?" asked Gonzo, trying to be helpful. "I found a chocolate-covered beanbag for Fozzie in my closet."

"Oh, I don't know what to do," cried Kermit. "I wanted so much to make this the perfect party. How could I forget Fozzie's present?"

But Kermit didn't have any time to worry about it, because the doorbell was ringing. He knew it was Fozzie, who thought he was coming over for a quiet birthday dinner with Kermit.

"Shhhh!" Kermit warned. "Everybody be quiet!" When his friends were all hidden, he rushed to the door to let Fozzie in, trying to look as if nothing was going on.

"Oh, hi, Fozzie," said Kermit. "Come on in. Dinner's almost ready."

Fozzie stepped into the living room.

"SURPRISE!" yelled everyone, popping out of closets and hiding places.

Fozzie fell back and laughed with joy.

Each time he discovered another friend or another special treat that Kermit had arranged, he grew more excited.

It was truly a wonderful party, from the pin-the-nose-on-the-clown game to the coconut-and-banana-cream birthday cake.

The guests had a great time.

Kermit was so busy listening to the jokes and dancing that he forgot his worries about Fozzie's present.

But when Robin squealed, "Fozzie, aren't you going to open your presents?" Kermit felt bad all over again.

Fozzie received all sorts of neat gifts.

He got a glow-in-the-dark bow tie from Floyd, fake eyeglasses with a big rubber nose from Zoot, a box of honey granola from Janice, and a big picture of Piggy in a pink lace frame—from Piggy, of course. Even Gonzo's chocolate-covered beanbag made him smile.

"Thanks, Gonzo," he said. "I've never seen one of these before."

"Really? I have six of them!" Gonzo exclaimed happily.

"I'd like to thank everyone for being so nice to me on my birthday," Fozzie said when he finished opening his presents. "But there's something I especially have to say to Kermit."

Kermit gulped. "I'm sorry, Fozzie," he began. "I wanted to get you a gift, but I was so busy planning the party, I forgot."

Fozzie looked confused. What was Kermit talking about? A gift?

"Kermit," he said, "this whole party was your present to me!"

"Time for cake!" announced Piggy, bringing in the cake Kermit had made. It was covered with lighted candles.

"I'm going to make my wish right out loud," said Fozzie, beaming. "My wish is that you'll be my friends forever and ever."

Clothes Make the Gonzo

Gonzo buckled the last buckle on his galoshes, stood up, and looked in his dressing room mirror. No doubt about it. It was his best outfit ever.

By Randi Hacker

Illustrated by Richard Walz

In addition to the black rubber boots, Gonzo had on a pair of red-and-white striped tights, a big white shirt with purple polka dots, a pair of glasses with black-and-white-checked frames, and a green Robin Hood hat.

"You're a handsome guy!" he said to his reflection in the mirror. As he turned to try and catch a glimpse of his back, he heard a knock and then the door opened.

Scooter stuck his head in.

"Five minutes, Gonzo," he said. "Better get dressed."

"I am dressed!" said Gonzo.

"I mean, you'd better put on the clothes you're going to wear onstage," said Scooter.

"I'm going to wear this," said Gonzo.

Scooter shook his head. "You've worn some weird outfits on this show," he said, "but this one takes the cake."

He closed the door.

"I don't care what he says," said Gonzo to his reflection. "I think I look colorful!"

Gonzo turned off the light and walked out to wait in the wings.

"You look like Number One on the Worst Dressed List!" said Miss Piggy.

"Another bizarre outfit from the Gonzo collection of bizarre outfits!" said Rowlf.

"This is no time to tease Gonzo!" said Kermit. "Leapin' Lenny is in the audience tonight. We have to be our best!"

"Leapin' Lenny and Jet Lag are my favorite band," said Rowlf.

"Leapin' Lenny!" sighed Miss Piggy. "What a dreamboat! I'd better go powder my nose, as he will certainly want to go out for a late, romantic snack with *moi* after the show." She ran off to her dressing room.

Gonzo suddenly felt embarrassed. A rock legend was sitting in the audience and he was wearing an outfit that no one liked. He must look really bad! Maybe he still had time to change into something else.

"You're on, Gonzo!" said Scooter.

Too late. Gonzo took a deep breath and stepped onto the stage.

Once he was in front of the audience, he soon forgot about his outfit. He sang, danced, juggled telephones, and gave the best performance of his life.

And when it was over, Leapin' Lenny led the audience in a standing ovation.

On the way back to his dressing room, he saw everyone clustered around Scooter.

"Leapin' Lenny is on his way backstage!" Scooter said.

"There he is!" said Kermit.

"Gosh!" said Rowlf. "The guy who sings 'Thirty Thousand Feet and Climbing'!"

Miss Piggy went up to Lenny and smiled charmingly.

"I reserved a table for us at my favorite cafe," she said.

But Lenny didn't hear her. He walked straight up to Gonzo.

"Gonzo, my main blue man!" said Leapin' Lenny. "How about loaning me your clothes for my concert tomorrow night? I dig those threads!"

"You mean you want to borrow my outfit to sing in?" said Gonzo.

"Not borrow," said Lenny. "Trade."

Lenny offered Gonzo a Jet Lag T-shirt that said

THE

I'M TIRED

WORLD TOUR.

He also gave him some blue jeans with interesting holes, and enough tickets to his concert so the whole gang could go.

The next night, they all went to the concert. And when Leapin' Lenny jumped onstage wearing his new clothes, no one cheered harder than Gonzo!

The Great Dress Disaster

"Mirror, mirror, on the wall, *moi* is the fairest of them all," said Miss Piggy gaily. She was very excited, for tonight her favorite frog was taking her to a fancy ball.

By Andrew Gutelle

Illustrated by Richard Walz

Piggy went to the closet. Hanging there in all its glory was the most beautiful white satin gown, the one she had been saving just for this occasion.

Piggy stood in front of the mirror and held up the dress. "I really am pretty gorgeous, aren't I, mirror?" she laughed.

Suddenly, Piggy's smile turned to a frown. There, right smack in the front of the dress, was a teeny little black spot.

"This will never do," she said firmly.

Into the kitchen she marched. She grabbed a sponge and dabbed at the spot.

"Oh, no," she said, looking at the dress in dismay. The little spot had spread out and formed a blotch.

"This will not ruin my evening," she said determinedly. "I'll get this fixed in plenty of time."

Piggy hurried to the laundry room, tossed the dress into the washing machine, added some soap, and turned it on.

"There!" she said with satisfaction. "That will do it."

While the dress washed, Piggy took a shower. But as she was drying her hair, she heard a loud noise. KERCHUNK! KERCHUNK! KERCHUNK! it went.

It was coming from the washing machine.

"Eek!" screamed Piggy, running to the laundry room. As soon as she got there, she realized what had happened: She had set the controls for SUPERSCRUBBER instead of GENTLE. She grabbed the dress out of the washing machine.

Piggy looked at her watch. "Yikes!" she said. "Kermit will be here any minute!" She tossed the dress into the dryer and raced to the attic to find her sewing kit.

Frantically, Piggy searched through one box after another in the dusty old attic. Finally, she found her thread.

The bell for the dryer rang, and Piggy ran downstairs. She pulled the dress out of the dryer and put it on to see how bad the damage was.

It was pretty bad. It was ripped on the left sleeve, it had a hole in the side seam, and the hem was coming down. In fact, the whole thing was frayed and tattered.

And what was more, when she looked in the mirror, she discovered that her face was covered with dust from the attic.

"Mirror, mirror, on the wall," she screeched, "this is not a fairy tale! This is a horror movie!"

Dingdong!

Oh, good grief—who could that be, bothering her when she was in such a state?

Piggy sprinted for the door.

It was Kermit! Piggy was so frantic, she'd forgotten it was time for him to pick her up.

"Ulp," she said. "Hi." She wished she were invisible.

"Hi, Piggy," said Kermit. "You look great. I knew you would think of a wonderful outfit for the costume ball."

Piggy stared at Kermit. He was wearing a red cape and a shiny gold crown.

"A *costume* ball?" said Piggy.

"Ha, ha, ha. I mean, of course, a costume ball."

"I thought my frog-prince costume would be the best costume of all, but I have to hand it to you. That's one terrific outfit. But Piggy, what are you?"

"Me? Why, I'm . . . Cinderella. That's it! I'm Cinderella *after* the ball. My coach is a pumpkin again, I'm all in ashes, and I'm wishing my prince would come. And here you are!"

"Here I am," said Kermit. "Now, let's go to the costume ball and dance and have a good time and live happily ever after."

And they did.

The Floppy Hopper Dropper Stopper

By Richard Chevat

Illustrated by Richard Walz

"We have a problem with the rabbits!" Scooter cried as he ran up the stairs of the Muppet Theater.

"A problem with the rabbits?" Kermit repeated. "What rabbits?"

"The acrobatic rabbits," Scooter panted. "They can't perform."

"But they're supposed to go on in fifteen minutes!" Kermit shouted. "What's wrong?"

"We don't know," Scooter replied. "You'd better talk to them."

Kermit and Scooter hurried to the rabbits' dressing room. Everywhere there were long-eared acrobatic rabbits dressed in colorful tights and capes, doing somersaults and back flips and their warm-up exercises.

"What's wrong?" Kermit asked the head rabbit, whose name was Abbot.

"We lost our floppy hopper dropper stopper," replied Abbot.

"Your floppy hopper dropper stopper?" asked Kermit. "What's that?"

"It's sort of like a net," Abbot explained. "We can't perform without it."

"Well," Kermit asked, "where did you see it last?"

"At home," said Abbot the rabbit. "In our rabbit attic."

Kermit looked at Scooter.

"We'd better find a floppy hopper dropper stopper, and quick," he said. "Where do we keep the rabbit stuff?"

"With the other hop props—in the hop prop shop locker," answered Scooter, and he ran down the hall to look.

"I don't see a floppy hopper dropper stopper, but here's a bouncing bunny bubble bracket," yelled Scooter, looking through the locker. "And here are some kangaroo kazoos, and some three-toed tree toad foggy froggy joggers."

"Keep the kangaroo kazoos in their case," Kermit said quickly.

"But better bring the bouncing bunny bubble bracket. And keep looking! Only ten minutes left till show time!"

Then he ran off to look in Piggy's dressing room.

"Piggy, you've got to help me!" he cried. "I need a floppy hopper dropper stopper."

"A what?" Piggy asked.

"A floppy hopper dropper stopper!" Kermit shouted. "For Abbot the rabbit. It's like a net, and if I don't find it in seven minutes, the hares will hop home."

"Well, don't get upset," Piggy said in a hurry. "How about this?" She pulled something that looked like a net out of her closet.

"What's that?" Kermit asked.

"A hanging humming hummock hammock. Will it help?"

"I don't know," Kermit said, grabbing the hammock. "But thanks."

He ran out into the hall, and there was Gonzo.

"Gonzo!" he yelled. "Have you seen a floppy hopper dropper stopper?"

"No, but I do have this," Gonzo said, holding up a tiny piece of cloth no bigger than a flea. "The grasshopper magician gave it to me. It's a free-flying fly and flea free-er."

"Never mind," Kermit moaned, and he ran back to the rabbits' dressing room.

"Abbot," Kermit said to the head rabbit, "we've looked everywhere. We found a bouncing bunny bubble bracket, a hanging humming hummock hammock, some three-toed tree toad foggy froggy joggers, and and one free-flying fly and flea free-er. But there's no floppy hopper dropper stopper!"

"Oh, that's all right," said Abbot the rabbit. "We found it."

"You did?" Kermit cried.

"Yes, but we're missing something else now," Abbot added.

"What is it?" Kermit groaned.

"One of our musical instruments, the simple single thimble cymbal."

"We don't have one of those," Kermit said. "But I'll tell you what we do have."

"What's that?" asked Abbot.

"A frantic, frenzied froggy!" Kermit shouted.

And with that, he ran out of the room.

Fozzie Goes Overboard

One day, Fozzie switched on the radio to listen to his favorite
disk jockey, Friendly Fred.

"I have a letter from Sally," said Friendly Fred. "And she wants
to know how to be a good friend. Well, folks, a good friend
always says nice things and never hurts other people's feelings."

By Kimberly Morris   *Illustrated by Richard Walz*

Now, it so happened that Rowlf had invited some of his friends over that very afternoon to listen to a new song he had written. Fozzie made up his mind to follow Fred's advice and say lots of nice things to everybody there.

When Fozzie arrived at Rowlf's house, Miss Piggy opened the door. She was wearing a new hat. Actually, it was a very funny-looking hat. But Fozzie remembered what Friendly Fred had said, so he exclaimed, "Piggy! What a beautiful hat!"

"Do you really think so?" asked Piggy doubtfully. "I think it might be kind of funny looking. Maybe I should take it back to the store."

"No!" said Fozzie. "It's beautiful!"

Then Fozzie turned to Kermit.

"Boy, I sure am glad to see you!" he said. "No party's any fun at all without you."

"Gee," said Kermit, "I don't feel like much fun today. I have kind of a stomachache."

"Oh, no, you're lots of fun!" said Fozzie.

"I'll bet you got the stomachache from that strange cheese we had before, Kermit," said Scooter.

"Scooter," said Fozzie, "you are probably the most brilliant person in the world to figure that out!"

Scooter just looked a little oddly at Fozzie.

A few minutes later, Rowlf called everybody to the piano to listen to the new song.

Fozzie didn't listen very closely, because he was busy thinking up compliments to give Rowlf. But when the song was over, he clapped as loud and hard as he could.

Rowlf took a little bow. And then he asked Kermit, Piggy, Scooter, and Animal what they thought.

They all liked the song. But Kermit and Piggy thought it should have a few more verses. And Scooter and Animal thought the beat should go a little faster.

Fozzie thought it was just terrible that the others were criticizing Rowlf's song. He was determined that when Rowlf asked him, he'd only say nice things. But for some reason, Rowlf didn't ask him. He just thanked everybody, and then he went into the kitchen to get the refreshments.

Fozzie followed Rowlf into the kitchen. He was sure that his friend must be feeling very upset.

"Rowlf," said Fozzie, "don't feel bad. I think it's a great song. And if you had asked me, I would have given you lots of nice compliments."

"I don't feel bad at all," said Rowlf. "Now that everybody has told me what they think is wrong with my song, I can make it even better."

"But they're your friends! Aren't friends supposed to say only nice things?" asked Fozzie, feeling bewildered.

"Friends are supposed to say honest things," said Rowlf gently. "But in a nice way."

Suddenly, Fozzie understood. He saw that if he said a lot of nice things he didn't believe, then his compliments wouldn't mean much. And that was why Rowlf hadn't asked him what he thought.

"Rowlf?" said Fozzie.

"Yes, Fozzie?"

"I really did love your song. But— maybe it should go just a bit faster."

"Thanks, Fozzie, old pal," said Rowlf with a smile. "I really appreciate that."

Fozzie smiled, too. "And now, if you'll excuse me," he said, "I think I'd better tell Piggy not to keep that hat."

Forgetful Rowlf

Rowlf noticed it when he sat down at the piano to practice. He looked down and there it was: a string tied around his finger. Now, most people tie strings around their fingers to help them remember things, but Rowlf couldn't remember just why there was a string around his finger. He couldn't even remember that he *had* tied the string around his finger.

By Craig Shemin

Illustrated by Richard Walz

Rowlf left the music room and tried to find someone who might help him remember why the string was on his finger. First, he asked Kermit, who was cleaning the hall closet.

"Kermit," said Rowlf, "do you know why there's a string on my finger?"

"It's probably there to remind you of something," said Kermit.

"I know that," said Rowlf. "I just can't remember what. I guess I'll just have to ask someone else."

Rowlf then decided to ask Miss Piggy, who was watching television.

"Miss Piggy," said Rowlf, "do you know why there's a string on my finger?"

"No," said Miss Piggy. "Maybe you tied it around your finger to measure your ring size."

"I don't think so," said Rowlf. "I probably would remember that."

Rowlf saw Scooter running up the stairs.

"Scooter!" called Rowlf. "There's a string on my finger!"

"Not so loud, Rowlf," whispered Scooter. "Everyone else will want one, too."

Scooter disappeared through a door at the top of the stairs.

"This is really bothering me," Rowlf said to himself. "I won't be able to get anything done until I find out what this string is supposed to help me remember. I had better ask some more people."

Fozzie was on the front porch, reading his favorite joke book.

"Fozzie," Rowlf began, "do you know why this string is on my finger?"

"No," Fozzie said, "but if you hum a little of it, maybe I can try to sing along."

"Fozzie!" shouted Rowlf.

"Wocka, wocka, wocka," responded Fozzie.

Next, Rowlf went to talk to Dr. Bunsen Honeydew, who was working on an experiment in the basement.

"Excuse me, Dr. Honeydew," said Rowlf. "Do you know why I have a string on my finger?"

"No, but I am glad you asked me that question!" said Bunsen. "At Muppet Labs, we've been working on the new Muppet finger-string detecto set. My assistant, Beaker, will demonstrate."

"Me-me-me-me-me-me-me-me," said Beaker

"Now," said Bunsen, "if you'll just place your finger into this electronic finger-ometer . . . ."

"Never mind," said Rowlf. "I'll figure it out myself."

Rowlf walked into the dining room—and there was Gonzo, eating a sardine and pickle sandwich.

"Rowlf!" said Gonzo. "I'm glad you're here! Thank you!"

"For what?" asked Rowlf.

"Thank you for letting me use your finger," said Gonzo. "I tied a string around it yesterday, while you were taking a nap, to remind me to buy a Valentine's Day gift for Camilla."

"You're welcome," said Rowlf, "but why didn't you tie a string around your finger?"

"I tried it," said Gonzo, "but it's impossible! Do you know how hard it is to tie a string  around your own finger? I just couldn't do it!"

Gonzo then left to go shopping for Camilla's present, and Rowlf just stood there, looking down at the string on his finger.

"That string kind of looks like spaghetti," Rowlf said to himself. And suddenly, Rowlf realized that he was very hungry. He decided to have lunch.

"I guess that string did remind me of something," said Rowlf. And he smiled as he untied it.

Let Me Help!

Everyone was busy getting ready
for a big show at the Muppet
Theater, and Robin ran to the theater
right after school. There he found
his Uncle Kermit at his desk
backstage, writing on his clipboard.

By Craig Shemin

Illustrated by Richard Walz

"I'm here, Uncle Kermit," said Robin.

"Hi, Robin," said Kermit. "What can I do for you?"

"You said I could help you get ready for the big show tonight," said Robin.

"Hmmm," said Kermit. "I can't think of anything for you to do right now. Why don't you see if Scooter needs some help?"

Robin went off to find Scooter, and found him standing near the big red curtain.

"Hi, Scooter," said Robin. "What are you doing?"

"I'm going to put up a new curtain-pulling rope," said Scooter. "The old one is almost worn out."

"Can I help?" asked Robin.

"I don't think so," said Scooter. "I have to climb up really high. It's a little dangerous. You're not old enough yet. But thanks for asking."

Next, Robin walked over to Fozzie, who was kneeling on the stage and hammering on some boards.

"What are you doing, Fozzie?" asked Robin.

"I'm nailing in some loose floorboards," said Fozzie. "My mother always said I would be a big hit on the stage! Wocka wocka, wocka!"

"Can I help?" asked Robin

"Thanks for offering, Robin," said Fozzie, "but this hammer is pretty heavy. I don't think you're strong enough yet."

Robin walked away from Fozzie and looked for someone else he could help.

In the lighting booth, Dr. Bunsen Honeydew and his assistant, Beaker, were working on the lighting controls.
"Hello, there, young fellow," said Dr. Honeydew to Robin.
"Hi, Doctor Honeydew," said Robin. "What are you working on?"
"Oh, I'm glad you asked!" said Dr. Honeydew. "Beaker and I are installing some new, computerized lighting controls."
"Meeep-Meep Mee-Me-Me," added Beaker.
"Can I help?" asked Robin.
"I'm sorry, Robin," said Dr. Honeydew, "but the equipment is very technical. Beaker and I have studied a long time to learn how to use it. After a few more years of school, I'm sure you'll be able to do work just like this."
"Thanks a lot," said Robin as he hung his head and walked away. "Nobody thinks I can do anything! Nobody wants me to help them," thought Robin as he sat on the edge of the stage.

Along came Kermit and saw Robin sadly kicking his feet against the stage.
"What's the matter?" asked Kermit.
"I'm too little to do anything," said Robin. "Nobody is letting me help."

Just then, Doctor Teeth called over from the other side of the stage.

"Hey, Kermit!" he shouted. "Animal dropped one of his drumsticks through a hole in the stage, and we're all too big to reach it."

"I can help!" yelled Robin.

Robin raced over to the hole, which really was tiny, and reached down with his little hand and pulled out the drumstick.

"Hey, thanks, my little green friend," said Dr. Teeth.

"Thanks! Thanks! Thanks! Thanks!" added Animal.

"See?" said Kermit. "You're not too little to help out around here after all."

"I guess everybody can use a little help now and then!" agreed Robin.

Piggy and The Pink Tap Shoes

Walking down Main Street one day, Miss Piggy passed the window of Rollo's Shoe Store and caught sight of something pink, something shiny, something positively perfect.

By Harry Ross

Illustrated by Richard Walz

It was a pair of pink patent-leather tap shoes with pale pink ribbons.

"Oh, my!" she breathed, pressing her nose to the glass. "They'd be perfect for my act. And they only cost twelve dollars!"

Piggy ran all the way home and emptied out every one of her pocketbooks.

"Ten . . . eleven . . . twelve dollars exactly!" she cried. "Payday's tomorrow, so I can spend the whole thing on those beautiful tap shoes today." And stuffing the bills and change into her pink patent-leather purse, she started back to Rollo's.

But before she got there, she came across Gonzo sitting on the curb holding a bent wheel.

"Hey, Piggy," said Gonzo dismally. "What's happening?"

"I'm on my way to Rollo's to buy the sweetest little pair of pink tap shoes, and they only cost twelve dollars. Why are you holding that bent wheel, Gonzo?"

"It's from my motorbike. I busted it while rehearsing my new act: being shot from a cannon while doing a triple wheelie. I won't have the money to fix it until payday, but if I can't do my act tonight, I won't get paid, and if I don't get paid . . ."

Piggy looked down at her purse and thought of the pink tap shoes. Then she looked at poor Gonzo.

"How much do you need?"

"Five dollars," he said.

She reached into her purse and counted out five dollars.

"Gee, thanks, Piggy. I won't forget this."

"Maybe I can give Rollo seven dollars so he'll keep the tap shoes for me until I have the rest," she said to herself as she continued on to the shoe store.

Then she saw Kermit, holding a tiny kitten in his arms, coming toward her.

"Hi, Piggy. Where are you off to?" he asked.

"I'm going to Rollo's to leave a deposit on some wonderful tap shoes. Where did you get that cute little kitty cat?"

"I found her," he said. "She's a stray, and I know she's hungry. Too bad I don't have enough money to buy her some food."

Piggy thought of her tap shoes and then looked at the sweet little kitty cat.

"Here," she said, handing Kermit two dollars, "buy her some nice cat food."

"Thanks, Piggy, that's really generous of you."

"I know," she said, waving good-bye.

A block from Rollo's, Piggy passed the luncheonette. Who should she see inside but Fozzie, waving frantically to her.

Piggy went in to see what was the matter.

"I left my wallet at home," Fozzie explained. "I can't pay my check."

"Yes, you can." Piggy handed him her last five dollars.

As she walked out of the luncheonette, Fozzie called out his thanks to her, but Piggy scarcely heard. She was thinking of those tap shoes and the lift they'd have given her act.

"Oh, well," she sighed, "they probably would have pinched my toes anyway."

The next day, she walked by Rollo's and discovered the tap shoes were no longer in the window. Piggy ran inside.
"You sold them?" she cried.
"What can I say?" he told her. "I had a mighty eager bunch of customers in here first thing this morning."

Piggy walked out of the store and quickly wiped away a tear as she saw Kermit, Fozzie, and Gonzo heading her way.
"There you are!" said Fozzie. "We've been looking everywhere for you."
"We wanted to pay you back," said Gonzo.
"Thanks," said Piggy sadly. She knew it was too late for the tap shoes now.

Kermit handed her a box.
A shoe box.
A shoe box from Rollo's. And inside, nestled in pink tissue,

were the pink patent-leather tap shoes.
"Oh, my!" she cried.
"Thank you!"
"It's the least we could do," said Kermit. "You were there when we needed help, Piggy."
"I can't wait to to try them on," said Piggy.

Robin and The Most Beautiful Bug

"Okay, everybody," said Ms. Ribit, the nature counselor at Frog Scout camp. "We're about to start our big summer projects, and they're going to be really fun!

By Harry Ross

Illustrated by Richard Walz

I'm giving each one of you a special jar with holes punched in the lid. Each jar is for a specimen; a bug that you'll find, keep long enough to watch closely, and then set free."

She held up a big poster with pictures of bugs on it. "These bugs on top," she said, "are okay for you catch. The ones on the bottom are not. Everybody ready?"

"Ready!" said everyone excitedly. And no one was happier than Robin. His favorite part of Frog Scout camp was nature class.

The scouts split up. Some went to the pond, others went to the fields, but Robin preferred to be in the woods. He searched for bugs on leaves, on the ground, beneath rocks, and in old rotting logs. But each time he saw a likely bug, it skittered away before he could catch it.

At the end of the period, everyone except Robin had caught a bug.

"Cheer up, Robin," said Ms. Ribit. "Sometimes you find the best bugs when you're not even trying."

On the way back to his lean-to, Robin tried very hard not to try. Just as he was turning off the main trail, he saw something out of the corner of his eye. He knelt before a berry bush, and there, clinging to a branch, he saw a little green caterpillar.

"I guess it's better than nothing," said Robin. He carefully broke off the branch and placed it, caterpillar and all, into his jar. Then he held up the jar and stared at it. It wasn't a very special bug, not half as creepy as a centipede or as stinky as a stinkbug or as peppy as a leafhopper, but it would have to do.

Back at the lean-to, Robin showed the caterpillar to his bunkmate, who had caught a daddy longlegs spider.

"Well, I guess a caterpillar is better than nothing," said his bunkmate.

After the rest period, Robin took his bug to show to Ms. Ribit. Ms. Ribit was quite excited.

"Congratulations, Robin! You really hit the jackpot."

"I did?" said Robin.

"You certainly did. I'll tell you what to do. Put your jar on the shelf of your lean-to or someplace cool. When the caterpillar finishes eating all the leaves off that twig, then go back to the bush where you found it and bring it another twig to eat."

"Then what?" Robin asked.

Ms. Ribit laughed at Robin's puzzled expression. "Then do what any good naturalist does. Watch and observe and learn. You're in for a big surprise."

So Robin put the caterpillar on the shelf right next to his bunk. He watched every day as the caterpillar sat on the twig and ate and ate. Robin had never seen anything eat so steadily. When it had eaten all the leaves off the twig, Robin went back to the berry bush and brought it more food.

Then one day, the caterpillar stopped eating and started spinning some kind of thread. Robin ran to get Ms. Ribit.

"He's spinning a cocoon," she explained. "Your surprise is only two weeks away."

Soon the caterpillar disappeared altogether into a fuzzy gray bag. It was very still. In the days to come, Robin almost forgot about the caterpillar as he busied himself with other camp activities.

Then one morning about ten days later, Robin heard a *crunch-munch-munching* sound coming from the jar. The caterpillar was eating its way out of the cocoon. Only it wasn't a caterpillar anymore. In place of the small, plain caterpillar, out came a beautiful butterfly with the most delicate wings of black and gold.

"Look!" Robin said to his bunkmates. "Look at my bug!"

His bunkmates immediately came over to it.

"Wow," said one.

"That's the neatest bug of all," said another.

"Open the jar and touch it," said a third.

"No," said Robin. "I don't think that's a good idea."

"Robin is right," said Ms. Ribit when she came to see. "Its wings are still too soft and delicate."

In a little while, Robin took the butterfly out to the berry bush, set the jar on the ground, and unscrewed the lid.

"Well," said Robin, "I guess it's time to say good-bye."

The butterfly climbed up onto the rim of the jar. It seemed to be testing its wings—or was it waving good-bye?

"Thanks for letting me watch you. So long, beautiful bug!" whispered Robin, as the butterfly flitted off into the woods.

Animal's Way

It was a beautiful spring day, and Kermit, Piggy, Gonzo, and
Fozzie were going on a picnic.

"Me go too!" growled Animal.

"Yes, Animal, you, too," said Kermit.

So they packed their lunches and games and blankets,
and then they all climbed into Gonzo's car for a drive to
the countryside.

By Richard Chevat   *Illustrated by Richard Walz*

72

"Oh, Kermie, I know we're going to have a wonderful time," squealed Miss Piggy as they passed woods and farms.

"Me too!" growled Animal.

Gonzo parked the car by a large field. Then they spread out their blankets, and everyone took out the food they had brought.

"Mmm, food!" exclaimed Animal.

They ate and ate until no one could eat anymore. Except for Animal, of course. He was always hungry.

"Come on, Animal," said Gonzo. "Let's go for a walk. You can finish eating later."

"Okay," said Animal. "But me still hungry."

Off they went, following Gonzo into the woods.

"These woods sure are pretty," said Kermit, after they had been walking for a while.

"Yes, and they certainly are big," said Piggy, looking around.

"And they sure are dark," said Fozzie nervously.

"And we sure are lost," added Gonzo.

"Lost!" they all shouted.

"What do you mean, lost?" Kermit asked Gonzo. "I thought you were watching where we were going!"

"And I thought Fozzie was watching," said Gonzo.

"Me hungry!" Animal growled.

"Not now, Animal," said Kermit.

"Think, everyone!" said Piggy. "How can we find our way back to the car?"

"I know," said Gonzo. "Let's follow those birds. They seem to know where they're going."

"Yes, but we can't fly," Kermit said, shaking his head.

"Well, let's scream for help," said Piggy.

"No one will hear us," Kermit replied.

"Me hungry!" growled Animal.

"Not now, Animal," Piggy scolded.

"Well, let's tell jokes," Fozzie said.

"How will that help?" asked Gonzo.

"It won't help," answered Fozzie. "But it might make us feel better."

"Me hungry!" Animal growled, even louder.

"Please, Animal," Kermit pleaded. "Stop saying you're hungry!"

"Oh, we'll be lost forever. We'll never get back to the car," Piggy sighed.

"And all that food at the picnic," added Fozzie.

"Food!" Animal growled. "Me want food!"

And he began running through the woods, shouting, "Food! Food!"

"Wait, Animal!" Kermit shouted. "Come on, we've got to catch him!"

They all chased after Animal, who had disappeared into the trees.

"Let's follow the sound of his voice," said Kermit. They could hear him shouting, "Food! Food!"

"Now we're more lost than ever," said Piggy as they trudged through the woods

"No, we're not." Kermit smiled. "Look over there!"

And there, beyond a clump of bushes, was the very field they'd started out from with Gonzo's car parked nearby. Sitting among all the picnic baskets was Animal, happily eating away.

"Animal, you did it!" they all shouted. "You found the way back!"

"Oh, I'm so happy!" said Piggy.

"Me not happy," said Animal.

"Why not?" asked Kermit.

"Food all gone!" Animal growled. "Hungry!"

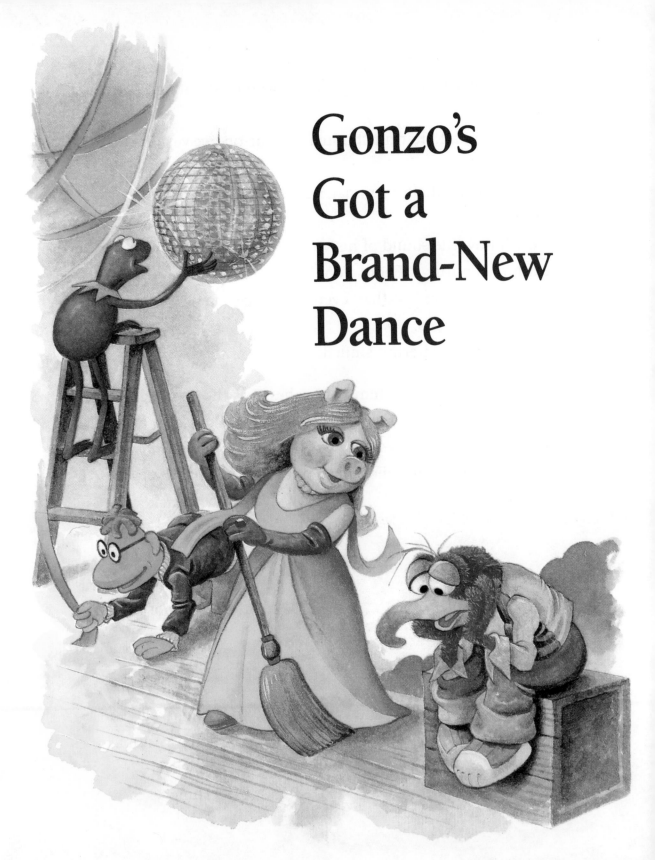

Gonzo's Got a Brand-New Dance

By Deborah Kovacs

Illustrated by Richard Walz

"Tonight's the night!" chirped Scooter as he draped crepe paper over the stage.

"Three hours to go!" hummed Kermit as he hung a glittering party ball from the Muppet Theater ceiling.

"We're going to dance all night!" sang Miss Piggy as she swept the floor. She pretended her broom was a handsome frog dressed in a tuxedo.

"Not me! I'm not going to be there!" said Gonzo from a gloomy corner where he sat, chin in hands.

Miss Piggy stood stock-still, shocked.

"*What??*" she said. "The Muppet Theater Ball is the biggest party of the year. Everyone will dance until dawn. I might even save a dance for you," she added, batting her long eyelashes.

"Don't bother," said Gonzo miserably. "I can't dance. That's why I'm not going to go."

"Can't dance?" snorted Miss Piggy. "Of course you can! *Everyone* can dance!"

"Not me," said Gonzo mournfully. "I have at least three left feet. I can barely walk across the room without sklonking myself in the ankle. It's hopeless."

"That's nonsense!" said Piggy with determination. "I'll teach you to dance—if you promise to come to the party."

"But the dance is about to start!" said Gonzo.

"I *love* a challenge," said Miss Piggy. "Let's go!"

Miss Piggy wrapped one of Gonzo's arms around her waist. She grasped his other hand firmly and held it up in the air.

"The first step is the waltz," she said. "Now, count along with me. A-one-two-three, one-two—*owwwwwww!*"

"Oh," said Gonzo, embarrassed. "Did I step on your foot?"

"Did you ever!" said Miss Piggy, rubbing her sore toes.

Miss Piggy tried to teach Gonzo the cha-cha, the rumba, and the tango. But his cha-cha was worse than his waltz. His rumba was worse than his cha-cha. And his tango was unspeakable.

Finally, Miss Piggy gave up. "I guess you're not a born dancer, Gonzo," she said. "But remember: You promised to come to the dance, anyway."

"I'll be there—next to the wall," he said sadly.

That evening, the party was crowded and lively. The dance floor was filled with couples in all their finery, swaying to the music of Fearless Frank's Caroling Cockatoos.

Gonzo huddled next to the wall, tugging at his bow tie. "I wish I were home," he thought miserably.

He was just about to leave when the band launched into its big hit, "When the Red, Red Robin Comes Bob, Bob, Bobbin' Along."

Gonzo perked up. "That's my favorite song!" he said.

At first, Gonzo just whistled along with the music. Then, his toes began to tap and his shoulders started to shimmy. Soon, his head was bobbing from side to side.

"Whoopee!" he shouted, running onto the dance floor. "That tune is the greatest!"

He twirled.

He hopped.

He skipped.

He sprang from one end of the room to the other.

He couldn't stop! At the end of the song, he sat down, totally out of breath.

"Gonzo!" said Miss Piggy. "You were just fooling me! You're a great dancer!"

"I am?" said Gonzo, shocked.

"What do you call that dance?" asked Miss Piggy. "You must teach it to me."

Gonzo thought for a minute. "It's 'Gonzo's Hip-Hop, Clip-Clop, Bop-Till-You-Drop Dance,' " he said, holding out his hands. "Will you dance with me?"

"And how!" said Miss Piggy.

All the party goers begged to dance with Gonzo. Soon, everyone was bouncing, leaping, twirling, and rocking, just like him.

And everyone agreed that Gonzo's Hip-Hop, Clip-Clop, Bop-Till-You-Drop Dance made that Muppet Theater Ball the best one ever.

The Really Truly Boffo Birthday Cake

"Tomorrow is Kermie's birthday," Miss Piggy said to Fozzie Bear. "We had better get everything ready for the party. I'll bake the cake. . . ."

"You *always* get to make the cake," said Fozzie. "Couldn't I bake it this time?"

By Harry Ross

Illustrated by Richard Walz

"Of course," said Piggy. "I didn't know you knew how to bake, Fozzie."

"Baking is a piece of cake," Fozzie said as he opened a cookbook. "All you have to do is follow the recipe."

"Actually," said Piggy, "it's not quite as simple as that. But if you start out with something easy, you should do just fine. Look, here's a nice recipe for cupcakes."

"Cupcakes are boring," Fozzie said. "Kermit deserves something special, and I'm going to make him a Really Truly Boffo Birthday Cake."

Fozzie continued to flip through the cookbook until he found what he was looking for.

"Here's a great recipe," he cried. "It's called Chiffon Whipped Dream Cake. Wow! It has five layers, four different kinds of filling, and something called lemon foam icing."

"Gee," said Piggy, "it sounds pretty complicated."

"Hah!" laughed Fozzie. "Any bear with a brain could bake this cake—just you wait and see!"

"All right," Piggy said with a shrug. "I'll see you here tomorrow for the party. And good luck with that cake."

The next morning, Fozzie woke up early so he could get started on Kermit's birthday cake. He reread the recipe, which was three pages long.

"Sift flour, baking powder, salt, and baking soda together,"
he read.

"Soda?" he wondered aloud. "I wonder what flavor?"

Kermit liked cherry cola, so he poured in some cherry cola.

"Separate six eggs and beat until fluffy," the recipe told him.

So Fozzie dumped six eggs into six separate bowls and got a
hammer and beat them until the shells were all mashed up

with yolks. The only problem was,
they didn't look fluffy. Fozzie tried
hard to find something to make the
eggs fluffy.

"Cotton? Pillows? No," said
Fozzie. He searched the kitchen
cupboards until he found a bag of
marshmallows. "This should make
them nice and fluffy," he said as he
poured the marshmallows in with
the eggs.

Then he had to squeeze the lemons. He held a lemon in each
fist and squeezed as hard as he could. Nothing much
happened, so Fozzie just tossed them into the bowl along with
everything else. Then he poured the batter into five cake tins
and put them in the oven to bake while he worked on the
fillings and the lemon icing.

"Baking's hard work," he said. "But it'll be worth it."

Three hours later, Fozzie wasn't so sure. Any minute now the
birthday frog and all the guests would be arriving, and the
kitchen was a mess, he was a mess, and the Really Truly Boffo
Birthday Cake was worse than a mess.

"I don't get it!" Fozzie cried when Piggy arrived early to check out the cake. "I followed the recipe."

"Don't feel bad," said Piggy, looking at the strange thing on the cake platter. The five layers were lumpy and lopsided. The four kinds of filling had all run together into one goopy kind, and the lemon foam icing looked more like green slime.

"This was suppose to be boffo," said Fozzie, "but it's just yucko."

"It does look kind of swampy. Hey! That's it!" said Piggy. "Let's just call it Swamp Cake and serve it anyway."

When Fozzie brought out the cake and Kermit saw the candle flames dancing in the pile of green slime, he cried out, "Swamp Cake! Just what my mother always used to make me!"

But it did not taste like what Kermit's mother used to make—not at all.

Everyone tried a little piece and politely said things like, "This has a very interesting flavor," or "This is certainly something."

"Don't worry," Fozzie said. "I know it's not very good, but tomorrow, after I clean up, I'm going to begin practicing how to bake. I'll start with something easy, like cupcakes. And by next year, Kermit, I'll be ready to make you a Super Duper Really Truly Boffo Birthday Cake!"

Robin and
The Haunted House

By Harry Ross

Illustrated by Richard Walz

Every afternoon when Robin and his friends walked home from school, they had to make it past the haunted house. At least, that's what it looked like.

Rising up out of the weedy lot at the corner of Downing and Poplar, it was a rambling old wreck with a sagging porch and shutters that banged eerily in the wind.

Just before they came to the corner of Downing and Poplar, they always crossed to the other side of the street, put their heads down, and ran like the wind until they were well past the haunted house.

"Otherwise," Robin's friend Samantha liked to say, "the witch will reach out and grab you."

For who else but a witch would be living in such a creepy old house?

One blustery afternoon, as the friends came upon the fateful corner, Tommy said to Robin, "I dare you to go up on the porch of the haunted house . . . and knock on the front door."

Robin handed his books to Tommy, squared his shoulders, and, while the others watched from behind a tree, crossed the street.

Creak!

He opened the front gate. If the witch hadn't seen him coming, she'd certainly have heard him. Slowly, he walked up the front walk. On either side, weeds choked what had once been a very nice garden.

Creak! Creak! Creak!

Up the sagging front steps he crept. He lifted a trembling hand to knock on the front door, when it opened before him seemingly all by itself!

"Yikes!" Robin started to run. But then, a sweet little voice called out.

"Why, good afternoon, young man."

Robin saw a teeny-tiny, wrinkled old lady dressed all in black. She was so old, she was no bigger than Robin himself. But her eyes were black and lively and her cheeks a rosy red. This lady was certainly not a witch!

"What can I do for you?" she asked.

Robin stammered. What could he say? That he had come to her front door on a dare? That he and his friends thought she was a witch?

"My friends and I thought you . . . might need a hand around the house with the chores."

The old woman clapped her hands happily.

"It just so happens I have quite a few chores that need doing. I'm all alone now and can't do things for myself the way I used to. Tell your friends across the street not to be so shy."

Robin turned and signaled to the others, who were still hiding behind the tree.

One by one, they ventured across the street.

That day, and every day after school for the next two weeks, Robin and his friends did chores for Mrs. Bigelow.

They weeded her garden.

They mended the gate and the porch railing and gave them a new coat of paint.

They even nailed back the banging shutters.

Every day the house looked a little less spooky and a lot more cozy. And Mrs. Bigelow, as happy to have the company as the help, made them peach cobbler and hot apple cider.

Finally, the house was all done.

And from then on, when they passed the house on the corner of Downing and Poplar, the children no longer put down their heads and ran for their lives.

Instead, they called out their greetings in bright, cheery voices to Mrs. Bigelow, who could sit on her porch now that it was fixed. And Mrs. Bigelow would call back, "How about some peach cobbler, children? Hot from the oven!"

And it was very good peach cobbler, too.

Forget It, Kermit!

Kermit was a very busy frog. Tomorrow night was the big talent show, and he was master of ceremonies. That meant he had about a million things to do.

"Miss Piggy," he said worriedly, "my library book is due tomorrow. Would you please remind me to return it before the show? I've got so much on my mind, I'm afraid I'll forget."

By Kimberly Morris   *Illustrated by Richard Walz*

"Gee, Kermie, I'm pretty busy myself," said Piggy. "I'm in charge of wardrobe," she added, trying to pin a slippery costum— —Scooter. "But I know how important it is to return —on time, so I'll try to remind you."

—gy," Kermit sighed. Then he hurried away, his —ed beneath his arm.

—iggy to Scooter, "I just hope I don't forget. —u please make an entry in your computer to —member to remind Kermit to return his book to

—ssured her. Then he squirmed out of his —ff to find Rowlf, who had promised to help —to sing.

—ter as they sifted through piles of sheet —ase put a note on your piano to remind you —ind Piggy to remember to remind Kermit —the library?"

—he rummaged through his trunk of songs. —d out to the bear, who was trying very —act, "will you jot a memo on your joke- —emind you to remind me to remind —to remember to remind Kermit to —rary?"

"You bet," said Fozzie as he accidentally-on-purpose slipped on his imitation banana peel and landed at Animal's feet.

"Funny!" bellowed Animal, clapping.

"Thanks," said Fozzie. "Hey, Animal, will you remind me to remind Rowlf to remind Scooter to remind Piggy to remember to remind Kermit to return his book to the library?"

"Remind Fozzie! Remind Fozzie!" roared Animal.

But in all the excitement, Animal forgot to remind Fozzie.

And nobody remembered to remind anybody to remember to do anything.

The next night, after the curtain had come down on the last act, Kermit suddenly remembered that he had not taken his book back to the library.

"Oh, Kermit," mourned Miss Piggy. "It was all my fault. Can you ever forgive *moi*?"

"It was all my fault," said Scooter. "I feel just terrible."

Rowlf and Fozzie felt terrible, too.

And Animal felt worst of all.

"Gee," said Fozzie, "we're sorry, Kermit. We'll all pitch in to pay the fine on your overdue library book."

"Gosh, no!" said Kermit. "That wouldn't be right at all. I checked the book out of the library and it was my responsibility to return it on time. But thanks for trying, everybody."

So the next day, Kermit took the book back to the library and paid the five-cent fine.

"Next time," he said to himself, "I'll remember to remind myself."

The Secret Admirer

Kermit, Fozzie, Rowlf, and Gonzo were eating lunch at Piggy's house one day when the doorbell rang.

"Excuse me," said Piggy as she went to answer the door. When she returned, she was carrying a huge basket of flowers.

By Susan Dias-Karnovsky

Illustrated by Richard Walz

92

"Aren't they gorgeous?" she sighed.

Piggy put the basket down on the table so her friends could admire the flowers. And that's just what everyone did.

"Oooh," said Gonzo.

"Aaah," said Kermit.

"Aaah-*choo*," said Fozzie, who was allergic to roses.

"Bless you," said everyone.

"Golly, Piggy," said Rowlf, "I didn't know it was your birthday. Why didn't you tell us?"

"It isn't my birthday," said Piggy, smiling.

"It isn't?" asked Gonzo. "Then why did someone send you flowers?"

Piggy smiled again.

"Because someone likes me," she said. Then she went to the kitchen to get some more sandwiches.

Rowlf leaned over to smell the flowers.

"I wonder who sent these?" he said, sniffing the beautiful scent.

"Aaah-*choo*!" said Fozzie, sneezing so hard that he lost his balance. He fell onto the basket, which caused it to slide off the table. Luckily, Rowlf and Kermit caught the basket before it landed on the floor, and the only thing that fell out was a little white envelope.

Rowlf picked up the envelope and read it. "It says, 'To Piggy,'" he said.

"I wish we could open it," said Fozzie, blowing his nose. "I'm *so* curious."

"It would be wrong," said Kermit. "But I'm curious, too."

"I know," said Rowlf. "We don't have to open the envelope. We could check it for fingerprints and then match the fingerprints to likely suspects."

"Or," said Gonzo, "we could check the flowers for clues. Like footprints."

"Maybe we could accidentally hold it up to the light, so we could see the writing inside," said Fozzie.

Just then, Piggy walked back into the room. She saw Gonzo holding the envelope, but she didn't say anything. She just giggled to herself.

At last she turned to her friends.

"You can open that envelope if you want," she said. "It's from my secret admirer."

"Secret admirer?" they all said at once. They waited breathlessly as Gonzo tore open the envelope and read the card out loud.

"It says," said Gonzo, scratching his head, "'To Piggy. Love, Piggy.'"

There was a moment of silence while everyone stared at Piggy, amazed. She just stood there, looking pleased with herself.

"You sent yourself flowers?" asked Kermit.

"But of course," Piggy replied. "I love flowers. They make me happy. Besides, I'm with me more than anyone else is. It would be sad if I didn't think I was wonderful."

Kermit smiled. "Makes sense to me," he agreed.

Rowlf nodded. "You know, it's actually a very nice idea," he said.

Piggy smiled, her pretty blue eyes twinkling. "I'm glad you agree," she said. "I think we should all send ourselves flowers sometimes."

"Ah-ah-aaaah-*chooo*!" sneezed Fozzie. "It's a wonderful idea, but I think I'll send myself a—ah-*choo*!—fruit basket instead!"

Shipwrecked

For weeks, Kermit and Fozzie had been planning their vacation at Salty-by-the-Sea Seaside Resort. As their taxicab pulled up to the hotel with its giant plastic model of Salty the Seal on the roof, they could hardly wait to get settled in and start their vacation.

By Harry Ross

Illustrated by Richard Walz

A swimming pool and shuffleboard and a smooth, sandy beach were all just waiting for them. But first, Kermit wanted to go out in a sailboat.

"Frogs make great sailors," he told Fozzie confidently.

They got their gear and went to the boatyard, where they rented a nifty little sailboat from an old salt named Skipper. Kermit put up the sails, tightened the lines, and off they glided.

"This is the life!" they agreed, as they settled back to soak up the sunshine.

After what seemed like hours, the water began to get a little choppy. Then it got a little more choppy. Fozzie turned a pale shade of green. Kermit turned a rather dark shade of green.

"Okay, I guess we'd better head back," Kermit said, turning greener by the second.

But as Kermit began to sail for the hotel, a thick fog moved in. In minutes, everything, including the hotel and Salty the Seal, was completely covered by a thick blanket of fog.

"Which way is the hotel?" Fozzie asked in a small voice.

"Gee," said Kermit, scratching his head. "I'm not sure anymore. Over that way . . . toward that big, dark shadow over there?"

"You mean toward that—that thing that looks like a sea monster?"

"Fozzie, there's no such thing as a sea monster." But just in case, Kermit turned the sails in the opposite direction.

Crack! A bolt of lightning lit up the sky.

"Oh, no!" Fozzie wailed. "What next?"

What happened then was that the waves swelled even higher, slapping against the sides of the boat and drenching them to the skin.

"Hold on tight!" shouted Kermit as a humongous wave lifted their boat high and hurled them into the air.

They landed on the sand with a bump!

Fozzie scrambled off the boat and up to the nearest palm tree, which he hugged with all his might.

"Where are we?" asked Kermit, peering through the fog.

"I'll tell you where we are," said Fozzie. "We're lost."

"Shipwrecked!" exclaimed Kermit.

"Marooned," Fozzie agreed, "on a desert island."

"Gee, well, I guess we'd better make the best of it, eh?" asked Kermit.

First, he got some canvas from the boat and rigged up a shelter. Then, he gathered driftwood and built a cozy fire.

Fozzie picked berries and dug up clams.

For dinner, they had clam chowder, and for dessert, fresh berries. Afterward, they settled down to sleep to the lulling lapping of the waves.

The next morning, the fog had lifted.

After a breakfast of coconuts, they collected shells and later they found some ripe pineapples for lunch. While Fozzie cut up the pineapples with a razor clam, Kermit lit a fire.

"It's to signal a passing ship," he explained.

It was midafternoon when they spied the boat just beyond the breakers. Kermit waved his arms. As the boat neared shore, they saw that its navigator was none other than Skipper from the boatyard!

"We're saved!" Kermit cried, jumping up and down.

"Saved?" Skipper asked, coming ashore. "From what?"

"Aren't we marooned on a desert island?" Fozzie asked.

Skipper laughed and led them on a very short walk around the point—and there, what did they see but the hotel, with Salty the Seal on the roof!

The two friends looked at each other.

The sea monster they had seen in the fog had been none other than Salty! All this time they had been right down the beach from their hotel.

Fozzie grinned. "Hey! It was great fun, anyway. More fun than shuffleboard, I'll bet."

"Oh, yeah?" Kermit laughed. "What do you say we go back to the hotel and play a few quiet games—just to make sure!"

The A-B-Seas

Kermit has settled into a deep sleep, deeper than the deep blue sea. He's having a wonderful dream about diving in the cove off Salty-by-the-Sea Seaside Resort. There he finds a treasure of alphabet letters that spell out his name:

KERMIT

Look at the picture. See if you can find the hidden letters that spell out Kermit's name.

Robin Takes a Hike

Robin was worried. He had to do his homework for school, but he was having a hard time settling down to work at his Uncle Kermit's house. It was a noisy place.

By Deborah Kovacs

Illustrated by Richard Walz

Just about everybody was over for the afternoon.

In the living room, Fozzie Bear was very loudly telling some new jokes.

Miss Piggy was using a hair dryer in another room.

Scooter was tinkering with a motor in the basement.

Even Uncle Kermit was making a lot of noise as he sat on the front porch strumming his banjo.

"I'll never get any work done here," thought Robin. So he packed his green knapsack, and off he went to look for someplace that was less noisy than home—a quiet place where he could do his homework.

Robin walked and walked. He crossed bridges. He waded through ponds, holding his knapsack high over his head. Finally, he found a quiet place under a beautiful willow tree. He looked around to make sure there were no giants or unfriendly creatures nearby. He saw he was alone.

"This place is perfect," he said.

He sat in the peaceful shade of the willow and took out his school supplies.

"Ah, nice clean notebook paper," he said. "And two sharp new pencils." He listened. "There's no noise here but the rustling of leaves and the buzzing of insects," he said happily. "I'll get my work done in no time!"

Robin picked up a pencil and began to write. "A book report on *The Three Bears*," he wrote.

Then he stopped to think. He thought and thought. But he could not think of a single other thing to write!

So he drummed his fingertips on his clean notebook paper.

And he drew circles with his sharp new pencils.

For what seemed like hours, Robin sat in that peaceful place, staring at his notebook paper, unable to write. Finally, he couldn't stand it anymore.

"Sometimes, things can be too quiet. There's only one place I can go to write this book report," said Robin as he packed up his knapsack again.

Once more he walked and walked. He crossed bridges. He waded through ponds holding his knapsack high over his head.

"I hope I get there soon," he thought.

Finally, he was there—back at his Uncle Kermit's house. It was still noisy, but he didn't care.

"I'm so glad I'm home. It's the best place to work," Robin said to himself. "It's where I feel most comfortable—even when it gets a little noisy. I'll just think a little harder and then I'll be able to work just fine."

Everybody was out on the porch. Kermit plunked his banjo, and everybody sang.

And when Robin had finished his homework, he went outside to join in.

A Hike in the Woods

Robin is taking a hike in the woods. But what's this? This isn't any ordinary forest. It's the "A" Forest. If Robin looks around, he'll find lots of things that start with the letter A. Can you find them, too? Here's what to look for:

Apples
Alligator
Airplane
Address

Alphabet soup
Armchair
Antlers
Ax

Ape
Armor
Ants

The Golden Banana

"**W**ant to listen to my speech?" asked Fozzie eagerly.

"What speech?" asked Kermit, who had dropped by Fozzie's house to borrow some sugar.

By Harry Ross

Illustrated by Richard Walz

"My acceptance speech," explained Fozzie. "It's what I'm going to say when I win the Entertainer of the Year Award. I've been working so hard on my act all year, I just know I'm going to win the prize tomorrow night. So I've got my speech all ready."

"Sure, I'll listen to your speech," said Kermit. "But, Fozzie, are you sure you're going to win? I mean, there are a lot of really good entertainers out there. Even though I think you're the most wonderful of all, you never know what the judges are going to do. Maybe you shouldn't count your chickens before they're hatched—even if they're rubber chickens."

But Fozzie was too excited to listen.

The next night was the awards dinner. Everybody who was anybody was there. Fozzie was so nervous he could hardly eat.

After dessert, Statler, who was head judge, stepped up to the microphone. "Ladies and gentlemen," he said. "Silence, please."

The audience whispered excitedly.

"It gives me great pleasure to announce this year's Entertainer of the Year," said Statler.

Fozzie blushed.

"It wasn't easy picking this year's winner," said Statler.

"Of course not," whispered Fozzie modestly to Kermit.

"So many talented performers," Statler went on.

"Shucks," said Fozzie, getting ready to stand up.

"But we finally narrowed it down to one very special talent," said Statler. Fozzie rose to his feet.

But Statler wasn't looking in his direction.

"The winner is Sarsaparilla the Shimmying Snake!" he announced.

Sarsaparilla was so surprised, she almost forgot to go up to the stage and get her award. And Fozzie was so surprised, he sank into his chair and just sat there, blinking.

At last, the truth sank in. He hadn't won. Sarsaparilla had won. She really did have a great act, and Fozzie knew it.

Everyone was clapping, and Fozzie began to clap, too. Then Fozzie got to his feet, clapping even louder for his friend Sarsaparilla who had worked so hard all year. And when Fozzie stood up, the whole audience stood up as well.

After the ceremony, Fozzie was the first to congratulate Sarsaparilla.

"You deserve the award," he said. "You're the best shimmy-er in the business."

"Thankssss," said the snake. "This was ssuch a ssssurprise."

"It sure was," said Fozzie.

The next evening, Kermit called Fozzie on the phone.

"Could you drop by my house for a minute?" he asked the bear. "I have your sugar bowl, and I have something else for you, too."

"Sure," said Fozzie, though he didn't much feel like visiting.

When Fozzie arrived at Kermit's place, it was very crowded. Everybody who was anybody was there, including Sarsaparilla. Fozzie was very surprised.

"Quiet, everyone," called Kermit. "I have an announcement to make."

A hush fell over the room.

"We are here to celebrate a truly bighearted person," he said. "Fozzie, come over here and accept your award—the Golden Banana, for Best Sport of the Year."

"Speech! Speech!" his friends all cried.

"A funny thing happened to me at the ceremony last night," said Fozzie. "I didn't win, and that felt pretty bad. But now I realize it isn't the award that's so important. Good friends and good work are what's important. And I'm lucky enough to have lots of both. Thanks, friends! I'll cherish this banana always."

"Hooray for Fozzie!" shouted his friends. "The winner of the Golden Banana!"

A Very Special Party

Miss Piggy was planning a party, a very special party, just for Kermit and her. She wasn't going to invite anyone else.

"Won't Kermie be so happy?" she said to herself. "I'll have all his favorite foods! What a great party."

By Richard Chevat

Illustrated by Richard Walz

"Did somebody say party?"

It was Fozzie. He poked his head through the doorway of Piggy's dressing room.

"Yes," Piggy said. "A very special one."

"Great!" Fozzie said. "I love parties."

"But—but—" Piggy started to say. It was too late. Fozzie was gone.

"Oh, no," Piggy moaned. "My party for two!"

She ran into the hallway to try to catch Fozzie and bumped right into Gonzo.

"Fozzie just told me about your party!" Gonzo said excitedly. "I'm going to get my pin-the-tail-feather-on-the-chicken game." And he hurried down the hallway before Piggy could say a word.

"Oh, I hope they don't ruin everything!" Piggy said. And she went home and got ready for the party. She put up her swamp decorations and made lots of nice swamp food. Just as she finished, there was a knock at the door.

"Oh, I hope that's Kermie, and not everybody else!" Piggy said worriedly as she opened the door. Standing there were Fozzie, Gonzo, Rowlf, and Scooter.

"Hi, Piggy!" Fozzie shouted as he came in. "I brought my squirting carnation!"

"And I have my songbook," said Rowlf.

"I brought some cookies and cupcakes," said Scooter.

"Where do you want me to set up my game?" asked Gonzo.

Just then Kermit walked in, too.

"Hi, Piggy. Hi, everyone!" he said, looking around. "Hey, is that pin-the-tail-feather-on-the-chicken?"

"Yeah, I thought we could all play," said Gonzo.

Suddenly, Rowlf noticed the look on Piggy's face.

"Is something wrong, Piggy?" he asked.

"I think I know," said Fozzie, looking at the table set for two. "This party was just for you and Kermit."

"Gee, Piggy," Gonzo said quietly. "Why didn't you tell us?"

"I tried to," Piggy said.

"We didn't mean to spoil your party," said Rowlf. "We'll leave. You can use my songbook."

"And I'll leave my game," said Gonzo.

"Enjoy the cookies," said Scooter.

"Have a good time," said Fozzie.

And they all left.

"Now," Piggy said to Kermit. "This is the way it was supposed to be. Isn't this fun?"

"Uh, yeah, I guess," said Kermit.

Piggy looked at Rowlf's songbook. "It's kind of quiet in here, isn't it?" she said.

"Yes," said Kermit.

"And pin-the-tail-feather-on-the-chicken isn't much fun with just two people, is it?" said Piggy.

"And it's too bad everyone had to leave before they could taste this great swamp food," added Kermit.

Piggy thought for a moment. "Kermit, I wanted to make a fun party for you, but I just thought of a way to make it even more fun."

"What's that, Piggy?"

Instead of answering, Piggy raced to the door and flung it open. Fozzie, Gonzo, Scooter, and Rowlf were walking away slowly.

"Hey!" Piggy shouted. "There's something I forgot to tell you!"

"What is it, Piggy?" Fozzie called back.

"I'm having a party," Piggy said. "And you're all invited!"

Robin and His Hood

Robin and his next-door neighbor Binky played together almost every day.

They liked the same games.

They liked the same books, and their favorite one was the story of Robin Hood. Together, they often played Robin Hood out in Robin's backyard tree house. Robin was always Robin Hood, naturally, and Binky was his best friend, Little John.

By Harry Ross   *Illustrated by Richard Walz*

When they were tired of playing that game, they did jigsaw puzzles together at a table on Binky's porch. And then there were always the swings. They liked to swing as high as could be and pretend they were sea gulls soaring over cliffs and oceans.

They even liked the same snack—salt-free pretzels.

Then one day, Binky's mother got a new job in another town. Binky and his whole family had to move away. Robin and Binky promised that they would write to each other. But as Robin waved good-bye to his friend, he said sadly to himself: "There'll never be another Binky."

A week passed. Robin tried to play Robin Hood, but it wasn't the same without Little John.

He set up a table on the porch for his jigsaw puzzles, but it was boring doing them all alone.

As he swung on his swing, he felt like a sea gull, all right— a lonely, sad sea gull.

Later, he was sitting on his front porch chewing on a pretzel, when a car pulled into the driveway of the house next door. A little girl got out of the backseat. She looked about Robin's age. Robin couldn't believe his good luck. Here was somebody to play Robin Hood with, somebody to do puzzles with and swing on the swings with. A brand-new friend!

Robin ran inside, grabbed some pretzels, and ran next door.

"Hi," said Robin to the girl. "I'm Robin, and these pretzels are for you. Welcome to the neighborhood."

"Hi," said the girl, looking at the bag. "My name's Louise, and I'm really sorry, but I'm allergic to all wheat products."

"Oh," said Robin, and took his pretzels back home. All that day, he watched the moving van being unloaded. The next day, he invited Louise over to see his tree house and play Robin Hood. But Louise didn't want to be Little John.

"I'd rather be Maid Marian," she said.

But somehow, playing Robin Hood and Maid Marian just didn't feel the same as playing Robin Hood and Little John.

After lunch, Robin said, "Let's play on the swing set."

"Let's not," she said. Then she saw the jigsaw puzzle on Robin's porch. "Let's do that puzzle instead."

"Great," said Robin. "It's a real hard one."

But Louise was so good at doing jigsaw puzzles that she practically put the whole puzzle together herself. She didn't even need Robin. Robin got up from the table and wandered over to the swings.

In a while, Louise followed him. She watched him swing, and sighed.

"I wish I could swing," she said. "Swinging makes me dizzy."

"Why don't you pretend you're a sea gull?"

Louise got on the swing and began to pump. "I feel dizzy," she said.

"Just think about being a sea gull flying over the ocean cliffs," said Robin. "The wind is blowing your feathers. Your wings can carry you wherever you want to go. You're free!"

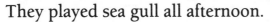

"Hey," Louise called out breathlessly, "I'm not dizzy anymore!"

They played sea gull all afternoon.

The next day, Louise gave Robin a present. "This is for helping me learn to love the swing."

Robin opened the present. It was a green hood, just right for Robin Hood.

"There might never be another Binky," thought Robin as he tried on his hood, "but this Louise wasn't so bad, after all."

"Let's play Robin Hood," she said. "I'll be Little John."

"You don't have to be," said Robin. "You can be Maid Marian . . . so long as she's willing to learn to swing on vines."

"I can do anything," said Louise, "with a little help from Robin."

Floyd's New Song

"Listen up, cats!" Dr. Teeth was trying to get the Electric Mayhem rehearsal started. "This is one big show we've got coming!"

Dr. Teeth wasn't kidding. The Mayhem was due to play the next night at the legendary Banana Bowl, one of the biggest concert spots in the area.

By Marianne Meyer

Illustrated by Richard Walz

It was hard to get Janice, Animal, and Zoot to stop talking about the show and start practicing. Floyd Pepper, the band's bassist, clapped his hands and called for everyone's attention.

"Cool out, scouts," said Floyd. "This show is gonna be big. In fact, I have composed a new song for the occasion." He demonstrated by singing a sweet, slow song that was as gentle as a lullaby. When he finished, all the band members applauded.

"Wow, that was mellow for sure," said Janice.

"Yeah, I can really sink my choppers into that number," said Dr. Teeth. He turned to Zoot. "What do you think, sax man supreme?"

"I dig it," said Zoot.

Even Animal had his own kind of compliment for Floyd.

"Good song! Good song!" he chanted, swinging from the rehearsal studio's overhead lights. "Let's play! Let's play!"

And so the Electric Mayhem began to rehearse Floyd's new song. Dr. Teeth started with a soft tinkling of notes from his keyboard. Then Zoot played a lovely saxophone line. Janice shook her tambourine gently, while Floyd plucked his bass for a low bubbly sound and began singing:

"Now that the night is falling,
I see the stars, the moon is calling—"

But then . . .

Crash! Boom! Bang! Animal jumped in with a furious pounding of the drums. Suddenly, the song didn't sound like a lullaby anymore. Floyd stopped the rehearsal.

"Lay back, Jack!" Floyd called to Animal. "This song calls for gentle drums, chum."

Animal didn't understand.

"Beat drums! Beat drums!" he yelled, crashing down on the set with his sticks. "Me drummer! Me beat drums!"

They tried the song again, but Animal came in at the same moment with the same loud crash and boom.

"Animal, my man," said Floyd, "lighten up."

Still, each time the band tried to play Floyd's new song, Animal pounded the drums loudly. Floyd was ready to give up when Dr. Teeth pulled him aside.

"Your song is groovy to the max," Dr. Teeth told Floyd. "But it needs a softer touch on the old drums."

Floyd sighed.

"I guess we have to drop the song, don't we?"

Dr. Teeth smiled, flashing his famous gold tooth.

"The Doctor has an idea," he said.

Floyd stopped worrying about his song, and the Electric Mayhem moved on to other numbers. The rest of the band rehearsal went well.

The next night, at the big Banana Bowl concert, the Electric Mayhem was terrific. They played all their greatest hits and the crowd loved them. As the concert neared its end, Dr. Teeth winked at Floyd and made an announcement.

"Ladies and gents, cool cats and cuddly kittens—we have a special treat for you. Presenting our main man, Animal, doing a super duper drum solo!"

Animal was delighted to be in the spotlight. He thrashed and bashed at his drum set with all his strength. He played six cymbals at one time while kicking the drums with his feet. Animal had never played so well—or for so long. By the time he finished his drum solo, he was exhausted.

As the audience cheered for the drummer, Animal lay his head down on a big drum to catch his breath. Immediately, Dr. Teeth gave a signal to the rest of the band and began Floyd's new song. Janice, Zoot, and Floyd came in with their parts, and the tender lullaby filled the air.

"Now that the night is falling,
I see the stars, the moon is calling
Oh, how I love the end of the day."

There was no crash and boom from Animal this time.

Floyd and Dr. Teeth turned to look at their drummer and smiled. After playing his solo, Animal was so tired that the gentle melody of Floyd's song had put him to sleep. He lay quietly on the drums, dreaming of the cheering crowd.

Floyd slid up next to Dr. Teeth.

"Can you believe, Steve? The cat's so cool he even snores to the beat!"

Hot Off the Presses

"Guess what, Uncle Kermit?" Robin shouted as he rushed in one day after school. "I'm the new editor of the school paper!"

"Congratulations, Robin," said Kermit. "I worked on a newspaper when I was your age, and it was a lot of fun. Newspapers are a great way to tell people things."

By Craig Shemin

Illustrated by Richard Walz

"I have only one problem," Robin confided to Kermit. "I'm not sure how to be the editor of a newspaper."

"Why don't you talk to your friends," Kermit suggested, "and see if they have any interesting story ideas for you?"

"Great idea, Uncle Kermit," said Robin. "That's exactly what I'll do."

And that's exactly what Robin did. The next day, he talked to all his friends.

"Does anybody have any news for my newspaper?" asked Robin.

"I have some news," said Willie. "I heard that Freddy Moore won't even talk to Maria Gomez since she lost his history book. He hates her!"

"Wow," said Robin. "They used to be best friends. That is big news!"

Robin spent the rest of the day gathering stories. When he got home from school, he sat down at Kermit's typewriter and wrote the articles for the *Tadpole Times.*

The next day, Robin and Mrs. Thatchwillow, the teacher who helped put the newspaper together, made lots of copies for all the kids. Then Robin handed them out to everyone he knew.

At lunchtime, Robin was eating his peanut-butter-and-jelly sandwich when Freddy walked up to him. Freddy looked pretty mad.

"Hey, Robin," said Freddy. "Why'd you write that stuff about me and Maria? Now she won't talk to me!"

Then a whole lot of other kids came up to Robin, all talking at once. "I didn't say I thought history was dumb!" said Jasmine. "Why did you print that in the newspaper?"

"I don't have a crush on Tony!" shouted Mary. "Now everyone thinks I'm silly!"

Robin felt like crying. He looked around at all the angry faces. Then he left his sandwich on the table and ran out of the lunchroom.

"Uncle Kermit," said Robin when he got home that afternoon, "I'm never going back to school again."

"Why not?" asked Kermit.

"Everybody says I put stuff that wasn't true into the *Tadpole Times*," Robin said. "Now my friends all hate me."

"Did you write things that weren't true?" asked Kermit.

"I thought they were true," said Robin. "Willie and Angie and Peter said they were true."

"Did you check and make sure?" asked Kermit. "Did you ask the kids you were writing about?"

"No," said Robin slowly, sitting down at the kitchen table. "I should have, huh?"

"Yup," replied Kermit.

Robin spent the rest of the afternoon writing a big letter for the front page of the *Tadpole Times*. In it, he explained that he had been wrong and said he was sorry.

The next day, Robin gave out his new paper. When he went to the lunchroom to eat his peanut-butter-and-jelly sandwich, his friends were waiting.

"I didn't mean to hurt anyone," Robin explained. "From now on, nothing goes into the *Tadpole Times* until it's checked out."

"That's okay, Robin," said Freddy. "We know you didn't mean any harm."

Robin felt a lot better. And that made his peanut-butter-and-jelly sandwich taste really good.

Fozzie Picks Fruit

By Deborah Kovacs

Illustrated by Richard Walz

"Fozzie," said Kermit, "there's no time to waste. Carmen Banana is on the show tonight, and she called to say that she needs some fresh fruit for her costume. Would you please go to Sneeden's Orchard and pick some apples and pears?"

"Sure thing, boss," said Fozzie, and he put on his hat and hurried over to the orchard.

Once there, he climbed a ladder into a big apple tree, its branches loaded with fruit.

"There's nothing like an apple," said Fozzie to himself, plucking one and putting it into his sack, "unless it's a lot of apples."

It was a hot day. After a while, Fozzie Bear took off his hat and put it on a branch. When he'd picked a few apples, he reached for his hat. But just at that moment, a big black crow flew past and grabbed Fozzie's hat in its claws.

"Oh, no!" cried Fozzie. "Bring back my hat!"

But the crow cawed and flew into the branches of a nearby tree, which was filled with pears. There it placed Fozzie's hat and flapped away.

Angrily, Fozzie climbed down the apple tree.

Fozzie climbed into the pear tree. His hat was up at the very top.

"First I'll get my hat," thought Fozzie. "Then I'll pick some pears."

His hat was pretty far up, and he had to stand on his toes to reach it. But finally, he got it and jammed it down on his head.

He picked a few pears until a big gust of wind came along, lifted his hat off his head, and blew it . . . into the apple tree!

"I don't believe this," said Fozzie.

He climbed down the pear tree. He climbed up the apple tree. He snatched his hat. He jammed it onto his head.

"There!" he said, reaching for an apple. "Finally, I can really get started!" But just then, he brushed his head against a branch and his hat fell off. "Oh, no!" he said, very annoyed. Then he looked at the ground.

"Oh, no!" he said again. A big brown stray dog was wandering through the orchard . . . and heading straight for Fozzie's hat.

The dog picked up Fozzie's hat and trotted away.

"Stop! Stop!" yelled Fozzie.

He climbed down the apple tree. He ran until he caught the dog, and after a little tug-of-war, he got back his hat.

"I'm pooped!" he said. He lay down under the apple tree and fell asleep.

In a little while, along came Kermit. He looked into Fozzie's fruit sack and found, to his surprise, just five apples and five pears.

"What on earth has he been doing all morning?" said Kermit, shaking his head. "I guess I have to do everything myself around here."

He grabbed the sack and climbed up into the pear tree.

"Golly," he said to himself. "Running the Muppet Theater sure has its ups and downs!"

Miss Piggy's Beauty Lesson

Miss Piggy sat at her dressing table, combing her hair. In just a little while, Kermit would be coming to take her to a lovely French restaurant.

"*Moi* must look very bee-yoo-ti-ful tonight!" sighed Piggy. She sneezed a tiny sneeze. "It's too bad I'm really not feeling well."

By Laura Hitchcock *Illustrated by Richard Walz*

Suddenly, she stopped. She stared at the mirror.

"Eeek! There's something on the end of my nose!"

Sure enough, right on the end of her (usually) perfect nose was a big, red, not-so-perfect spot.

"Oh, dear," Piggy sighed. "What can be wrong with me?"

Piggy tried covering the spot with bath powder. Her face turned white, but the spot stayed red.

She tried hanging a handkerchief over her nose. It looked stupid.

Finally, she ran to the phone and called Kermit.

"I'm sorry, Kermie! I can't make it tonight! I—uh, uh—have to wash my hair!"

"Gee, Piggy," he asked, "Can't you wash it later?"

"No!" shouted Miss Piggy. "I mean—ha, ha— it's just too dirty."

"Okay," said Kermit, but he thought Piggy sounded strange.

Miss Piggy went back to her dressing table. How awful if Kermie had *seen* that ugly red spot on her nose!

She glanced in the mirror again . . . and shrieked! Red spots now covered her entire face!

Poor Piggy. She was really feeling sick. But even worse—as far as Piggy was concerned—was the fact that her whole body, from ears to feet, was now covered with spots. And they itched, too! The spots were so ugly, Piggy decided to hide from everyone—forever, if necessary.

For days, she saw no one. When her friends invited her out—whether to the movies or the ballet—Piggy would not go. No one saw her . . . or her spots.

Meanwhile, Kermit was worried. Why was Piggy avoiding everyone?

Finally, he had an idea. He telephoned Fozzie Bear and Gonzo. Both of them agreed to meet Kermit at Piggy's house that night.

When they arrived, all was dark. Nevertheless, they joined hands outside Piggy's window.

"If we call loudly enough, she'll have to come out!" said Kermit.

"Pig-gy! Pig-gy!" they shouted.

Finally, a light went on inside. The curtain opened a crack, and someone peeked out.

"Come out, Piggy!" called Kermit. "We miss you!"

The figure at the window sniffed.

"I can't come out! I'm covered with spots and I'm ugly!"

"We don't care what the outside of you looks like," Kermit replied. "We care about the inside!"

Slowly, Miss Piggy opened the curtain all the way. At last, everyone would see those awful red spots!

Kermit gasped . . . not in horror but in surprise.

"Oh, Piggy, you're not ugly—you just have the chicken pox! I had that myself a few months ago!"

"Me, too!" said Fozzie. "The chicken pox is nothing to squawk about!"

"Oh, Fozzie." Piggy smiled a little. "Really?"

Gonzo added, "Yep! And even though you're feeling sick now, you'll be feeling a whole lot better in a couple of days."

Kermit agreed. "You just need a lot of rest," he said. "If you like, we'll even keep you company."

"We can't catch it 'cause we've all had it already," Gonzo explained.

"Hmm," said Miss Piggy. "Your offer sounds really nice to me!"

So they all came in. And though Miss Piggy was still covered with spots, she had a wonderful time. After all, she was with her friends!

All Work! All Play!

On a beautiful autumn day, Floyd Pepper, the coolest guitar player you ever heard, was sitting outside playing his brand-new tune: "*Thwang-a-thwang-a-thwang-thwang!*"

By Jim Lewis

Illustrated by Richard Walz

Floyd's song was so cool it made you jump up, wave your arms, shake your hips, wiggle your legs, and smile a big silly smile. Everyone who heard this song was happy. Everyone, that is, except for Sam the Eagle.

"Harrumph," harrumphed Sam, who was busy getting ready for winter. He was putting up storm windows, knitting hats, nailing down shutters, fixing roof shingles, toting barges, lifting bales, and generally working himself into quite a dither.

"Harrumph!" Sam harrumphed again. "You can't just fool around all fall, you know. If you play music all day, you'll freeze when winter comes!"

Floyd finished his song and looked up at Sam: "Sam, my man! Winter is no worry for me. See, if I play all day long, when winter comes I'll be warm."

"Ha!" exclaimed Sam the Eagle. "You should work, not play!"

"Sam, my man!" Floyd replied. "I am! I am! I'm working."

But Sam wasn't listening. He'd stormed off, harrumphing all the way. Floyd was sorry that Sam was gone, so he cheered himself up by playing his song: *Thwang-a-thwang-a-thwang-thwang!*

And everyone in the neighborhood jumped up, waved their arms, shook their hips, wiggled their arms, and smiled big silly smiles. Everyone, that is, except Sam.

This went on for weeks. Then one morning, Sam woke to discover that the first big winter snowstorm had come overnight. Snow was covering the roads, the trees, the sidewalks, the cars, and . . .

Gasp! thought Sam. Maybe it was covering poor Floyd Pepper!

Sam suddenly felt sorry for his guitar-playing pal.

"I tried to warn him, but he wouldn't listen," Sam thought.

So quick as can be, Sam gathered up blankets, hot soup, and all sorts of winter warming stuff and headed off through the deep, deep snow to save Floyd.

Sam ran into Floyd's house, but could find no sign of his friend.

"Oh, no," he thought. "The blizzard blew Floyd away! I'll never see him again! I'll never hear his happy song!"

But then Sam heard the most amazing sound: "*Thwang-a-thwang-a-thwang-thwang!*"

It was Floyd's song! Sam ran out to the road and found Floyd.

"You're all right," said Sam, hugging his pal right there. "Come inside!" he cried.

"Sorry, Sam, my man. No can do—but thanks for the offer."

Sam now noticed that Floyd was surrounded by stacks of luggage.

"Uh, where are you going with all that luggage?" he asked.

"To the tropics, Sam, where it's nice and warm," explained Floyd. "That's what I've been tryin' to tell you all this time: It really is work when I play my guitar. I've been practicing for this All-Winter Tropical Tour with my band."

"Uh, right," said Sam. "I knew that."

And just then, Floyd's band pulled up in the van. "Say, Sam, my man," said Floyd. "You want to tour the tropics with us?"

"Well, er," harrumphed Sam, "I just so happen to have some new suitcases."

In a flash, Sam was back with his bags packed.

Now, if Floyd and the band ever come to your town, here's how you can spot Sam: He's the only one who's not jumping up, waving his arms, shaking his hips, wiggling his legs, or smiling a great big silly smile. But he does look very happy— for Sam the Eagle.

Messy Gonzo

Gonzo was a messy guy. He wasn't just a little messy—a sock on the floor here, a few crumbs on the counter there. He was a *lot* messy. Gonzo was perhaps the messiest guy in the universe.

Actually, Gonzo liked things that way.

By Ellen Weiss

Illustrated by Richard Walz

He liked having all his shoes out on the floor; it made it easy to find the right pair.

He liked keeping his spoon collection in the bathroom sink.

He liked lots of old magazines on his bed; if he wanted to look at a copy of *Chicken World* magazine, or maybe *Weirdo Week*, it was right there.

Gonzo knew where every single thing in his house was. He had a system.

One Saturday morning, Gonzo was over at Miss Piggy's house, getting ready for the big spring picnic on Sunday.

Piggy was in the kitchen, making a chocolate cake. Fozzie was setting out all the plastic forks, paper plates, and napkins. And Gonzo had climbed up into Piggy's attic to get down her big picnic basket.

"Gonzo," called Piggy from the kitchen, "do you have any sugar in your house? I just ran out."

"Sure," said Gonzo. "I'll go and get it."

"It's okay," said Piggy. "You don't have to come down from there. I'll go. Where do you keep the sugar?"

"Right under the bed," said Gonzo. "You can't miss it."

So off Piggy went to get the sugar.

Four hours later, Piggy was not back.

"Gee," said Fozzie to Gonzo as they cut carrot sticks, "I wonder where Piggy is? Do you think she got swallowed up by the junk in your house?"

"I don't think any of it's alive," mused Gonzo, "but maybe I should go check anyhow."

So Gonzo went home to look for Piggy.

When he walked into his house, he thought he'd gone to the wrong one by mistake. This house was neat, orderly, and shining clean. Maybe it was Mrs. Prothero's house, next door.

But, no—there was Piggy, mopping the kitchen floor.

"Well," said Piggy, with a satisfied smile, "You certainly needed *moi* around here. I've just tidied up your whole house for you."

Gonzo was stunned.

"Um, thanks, Piggy," he said. "I think."

"You're welcome," said Piggy, putting the mop away.

"So, that's my kitchen floor," said Gonzo in wonderment. "I've never seen it. But, Piggy," he said, "what did you do with my rubber tire collection?"

"I put it out in the backyard," she said. "You don't need tires in your kitchen."

"Yes, I do," protested Gonzo. "I like them there."

Gonzo walked into his living room.

"Piggy," he said, "where are my jars of interesting fungus?"

"I put them in the basement," said Piggy with a shudder.

"But, Piggy, they're an experiment!" wailed Gonzo.

He ran to the refrigerator and looked in.

"Where are all my socks?" he cried.

"They're in your dresser drawer, silly," said Piggy.

"But that's where I keep my walnuts!" moaned Gonzo. "Don't you see, Piggy? I knew where everything was around here. I had a system. And now I'll never be able to find anything!"

"I was only trying to help," said Piggy, a little hurt.

"It was really nice of you, but I can't live this way. I need everything back the way it was."

"All right," sighed Piggy. "Let's get to work."

For the next four hours, they worked on Gonzo's house, putting everything back where it had been. It was hard work, but at last it was done, right down to the sugar under the bed

"Are you happy now?" asked Piggy, wrinkling her nose.

"Yes," grinned Gonzo, taking a walnut from his dresser drawer. "Very, very happy."

Spring Cleaning

Gonzo has a problem. He has a lot of things to clean up, and he has decided to sort them into three boxes. He's labeled each box with a *B*, an *S*, or an *L*. Can you help him decide where to put everything? With your finger, draw a line from each "B" thing to the "B" box. Then do the same thing for the "S" things and the "L" things. Thanks for helping Gonzo!

While Gonzo is cleaning up, he's going to get rid of some other things by selling them at a garage sale. Maybe you can give him some ideas for things to sell. Look around your own house, and see if you can find something that starts with a *T*, something that starts with a *P*, and something that starts with an *SH*. Have fun!

COME ONE! COME ALL! GARAGE SALE TOMORROW! GREAT STUFF!

Where's Beaker?

Welcome to
MUPPET LABS, the neatly
printed sign told Kermit.
STEP THROUGH THIS
DOOR AND JOIN OUR
INVENTORS IN THE
WORLD OF
TOMORROW.

Kermit pushed the
door open and stepped
inside.

By Andrew Gutelle   *Illustrated by Richard Walz*

Muppet Labs was a collection of odd gadgets and strange sights, but none was stranger than the one in the center of the room. It was Dr. Bunsen Honeydew, sitting on the floor holding a string. The other end of the string was connected to a garbage can on wheels. The can was covered with gears and lights. As Honeydew tugged on the string, the machine let out a loud noise: *Meeeep! Meeeep!*

"Hi, Bunsen," said Kermit. "What's that? A space-age trash collector?"

"No, this is my Beaker Seeker," replied Honeydew. "I invented it so that I could locate my friend and assistant, Beaker, at all times."

"How does it work?" asked Kermit.

"It's really quite simple. This machine makes a high-pitched noise that sounds just like Beaker. It then finds a matching sound here in Muppet Labs. Obviously, that sound must be made by my missing assistant."

"That's terrific," said Kermit. "By the way, where is Beaker, anyhow?"

Bunsen Honeydew looked around the room.

"That's odd. He was here a minute ago. Well, this is a perfect opportunity to test my invention."

Bunsen flicked a switch, and the machine began rattling and shaking and meeping. It rolled to a trunk in the corner of the room and stopped.

Kermit opened the trunk. Out hopped a tiny mouse, which raced between Kermit's legs and darted into a hole in the wall.

"Gee, Bunsen, your machine found a squeaker instead of Beaker," said Kermit.

"Maybe it needs a little time to warm up," suggested Bunsen. He flipped the switch again, and the can began shaking. "*Meeepeep! Meeepeeep!*" it shrieked as it rolled out the door.

Kermit and Bunsen ran after it. The machine bounced upstairs, meeping as it went. It rolled down the hallway and came crashing to a stop next to a locker. Bunsen opened it.

"Eureka!" he shouted.

"We found Beaker?" asked Kermit.

"No, but I found my rubber ducky," said Bunsen, squeaking the toy happily. "I've been looking for this for days."

"That's great, Bunsen, but your machine didn't find Beaker," said Kermit.

"Perhaps a small adjustment—" said Bunsen. He picked up a screwdriver and loosened the lid on the can. Suddenly the lid flew off. Out popped Beaker!

"Beaker, what were you doing inside Bunsen's invention?" asked Kermit.

"*Meep-meep-mee-mee!*" squeaked Beaker, happy to be free.

"Oh, my goodness! Now I remember," cried Honeydew. "In order for this device to work, I had to put something inside it that sounded like Beaker. What could sound more perfect than Beaker himself?"

"Gee, Bunsen, I guess your invention is a failure," said Kermit. "How can it find Beaker if he has to stay inside it?"

"On the contrary, how can it fail?" replied Bunsen. "As soon as I flip it on and it starts meeping, I'll remember exactly where my assistant is. Right, Beaker?"

"*Meeeepeeeep!*" meeped Beaker.

Fozzie's Costume

Today was Halloween, Fozzie's favorite holiday. He loved to see all the people in their funny costumes.

The whole gang was meeting at Piggy's house for a masquerade party. For weeks, Fozzie had been thinking about his costume, but he hadn't been able to decide what he wanted to be.

By Andrew Gutelle

Illustrated by Richard Walz

Fozzie took a walk that afternoon, hoping an idea would hit him. He didn't have much time left to come up with something.

On the corner, a clown with a bright red nose and big floppy shoes waddled up to him.

"Hi, Fozzie!" said the clown.

"Gonzo, is that you?" said Fozzie. "What a great outfit. I didn't even recognize you!"

"Thanks," said Gonzo. He took three bags of jelly beans out of his pockets and started to juggle them.

"Isn't it too early to go to Piggy's?" asked Fozzie.

"I'm going to pick up Rowlf first," explained Gonzo. "He's going to be a clown with me. Would you like to join us? We could go to the party as a three-ring circus!"

"Gee," replied Fozzie. "I don't know. Maybe I'll call you later, okay?"

"Sure!" Gonzo said. "See you at the party!"

Fozzie continued down the street.

"Gee, I wish I had an idea," he thought. Just then, Fozzie rounded a corner. Standing in front of him was a giant.

"Hi, Fozzie," boomed the giant.

"Who are you?" asked Fozzie.

"It's me," said Skeeter.

"And me, too," added Scooter, peeking out from the giant's shirt.

Skeeter was sitting on his shoulders. "And if you joined us, we could be a king-size giant!"

"Well, maybe," said Fozzie. "I'll have to think about it."

As Fozzie walked home, more and more people in costumes began to fill the streets. He saw cowboys, ghosts, monsters, ballerinas, and witches. And each time he saw a great costume, he had the same thought—"Gee, maybe it would be fun to be that."

Fozzie went home and paced back and forth in his bedroom. He opened his closet and looked in. He went to the kitchen and checked out all the cupboards. Then he just stood in front of the mirror, thinking.

And then, as Fozzie looked at himself in the mirror, he watched a wide smile come over his face.

"That's it!" he shouted.

Fozzie raced back to the kitchen and grabbed a roll of aluminum foil. Then he ran up to the attic, where he found an old picture frame.

Carefully, he stretched the foil across the frame, from side to side and top to bottom. Then he cut little holes for his eyes and held the frame up in front of him.

"Great!" he said with satisfaction. Off he raced to Piggy's house.

When he got there, the first person he saw was Gonzo the Clown.

"That's a great costume, Fozzie," said Gonzo. "What are you?"

"I am the world's newest superhero," said Fozzie proudly. "I'm Mirror Man."

Gonzo stood in front of Mirror Man.

"Gee, Fozzie, it looks to me like you're wearing a clown costume," he said.

"Precisely!" said Mirror Man.

"I see you as a cowboy," said Kermit, who was dressed like a cowboy himself.

"Correct again," said Mirror Man.

The other guests took turns looking at Mirror Man.

"Your costume is just like mine!" said each one.

"That's what's great about being Mirror Man," said Fozzie happily. "I can be a cowboy, a clown, a giant, or anything else at all. This is the perfect costume for someone who can't decide what he wants to be—like me!"

Swedish Chef, Private Eye

"Whoop-de-doo!" said the Swedish Chef as he hung up his apron. This had been a very long day in a very, very long week of a very, very, very long year.

By Jim Lewis
Illustrated by Richard Walz

154

But now the time had come for the Chef to go on vacation! He was traveling back to the old country to visit his favorite relative, Uncle Toodaloo.

Uncle Toodaloo, a great chef in his own right, had taught the Swedish Chef everything he knew about baking delicious pastries. Oh, Toodaloo could be a little forgetful—like the times he forgot where his bakery was, or the times he came to work in his pajamas, or the times he wore his dog as a hat. But when it came to making the very best tarts, pudding puffs, three-layer butterscotch cakes, pies, cookies, and doughnuts in the whole world, there was nobody better than Uncle Toodaloo.

"Yum-yum!" said the Swedish Chef as he walked up to Uncle Toodaloo's Yummy-You-Betcha Bakery Shop.

Ringa-ding-a-ding! rang the bell over the door as he entered.

"Ooncle!" cried the Swedish Chef.

"Nephoo!" shouted Uncle Toodaloo, and the two chefs hugged, hooped, hollered, and danced around the little bakery. But when they had finished saying hello, the Swedish Chef noticed that his uncle looked worried.

"Whoot's der matter?" asked the Chef. Uncle Toodaloo told his nephew that a very valuable cooking tool was missing from his kitchen—a one-of-a-kind fritter-smacker, which was used, of course, for smacking fritters.

"Ooh, my goosh!" said the Chef. This was a very serious matter: A baker like Toodaloo simply could not bake if he had nothing with which to smack fritters.

The Chef decided to try to solve this mystery, and he began at once. He started by using a bag of flour to dust for fingerprints, but this just made a big powdery mess.

He searched high and low, through cupboards and closets, but the fritter-smacker was nowhere to be found.

He talked to the chickens and rats who worked as Uncle Toodaloo's assistant bakers, but they had seen nothing suspicious. He even questioned the dog sitting atop his uncle's head (Toodaloo had mistaken his dog for a hat again), but the dog knew nothing.

The Swedish Chef shook his head sadly and apologized to his uncle. It looked as if the missing fritter-smacker was lost forever. Uncle Toodaloo thanked his nephew for trying, but he looked sad, too.

In a little while, however, Uncle Toodaloo remembered a surprise that he had baked for his favorite nephew. He brought out the most beautiful cake you could ever imagine. Written on top in creamy, sweet icing were the words WELCOME BACK, CHEF!

The Chef served everyone a slice. But when he went to eat his first bite of cake, his fork hit something hard.

"Ooh, my goosh!" the Chef said. There on his plate was the mysteriously missing fritter-smacker!

"Ooh, my goosh!" said Uncle Toodaloo, who had absentmindedly baked the fritter-smacker into his cake. "I goofed!"

Uncle Toodaloo was very sorry that he had caused all that trouble. But the Swedish Chef didn't mind. He was happy to be with his uncle, happy to be on vacation, and happy that he had, after all, solved the mystery of the missing fritter-smacker.

Robin's Blanket

Robin was excited. His friend Jeffrey was having a Frog
Scout sleep-over party, and they had big plans—staying up
late, playing leapfrog, telling ghost stories.

Robin took out his knapsack and tossed it onto the bed.
He'd never slept over at anyone's house before, and he wanted
to be sure he had all the right things. He searched through his
dark, crowded closet.

By Cheryl Gotthelf   *Illustrated by Richard Walz*

"Let's see. I'll need comic books, a toothbrush . . . and my flashlight so I can read under the covers."

But something was still missing. Robin looked all around the room.

"I know," said Robin. "I forgot my blanket!" He grabbed his fuzzy blue blanket with the faded green lily pad on it. He'd never slept without it before.

Robin shoved everything into his knapsack. He yanked on the zipper, but a big piece of the blanket stuck out, looking very silly. What if the other Frog Scouts made fun of him?

Suddenly Robin wasn't so excited about the party. He trudged down the stairs, dragging the knapsack behind him.

Uncle Kermit was sitting on the porch, playing the banjo.

"All packed?" he asked.

"I'm not going," muttered Robin.

"Why not?" Kermit asked, surprised.

"I can't go without my blanket. But if I bring it, they'll all laugh at me," said Robin.

"I see," answered Kermit.

Robin sat down on the bench swing and kicked his feet back and forth.

"You know," Kermit began, "I had a special pillow when I was a Frog Scout."

"Really?" said Robin.

"Sure," said Kermit. "Almost everybody has something special that makes them feel safe and happy."

Robin wasn't so sure. None of his friends would drag a dumb old baby blanket to a sleep-over. He still felt glum.

"Then again," said Kermit, looking at Robin's sad face, "a sleep-over party isn't everything. You *could* stay home." He patted Robin on the shoulder and went inside.

Robin thought and thought. If he went to the party, someone might tease him. But if he stayed home, he'd miss all the fun.

Finally, he stood up straight, slung his knapsack over his shoulder, and marched to Jeffrey's house without looking back.

Robin was the first to arrive.

"You get to pick where you want to sleep," said Jeffrey, taking his friend upstairs.

Robin climbed the ladder to the top of Jeffrey's bunk bed. Through the window, he could see down the block to his Uncle Kermit's house.

Jeffrey had tons of stuff in the bed—rubber bands, baseball cards, and stickers. In the middle of the bed, under the cover, was a big lump. Robin turned down the cover, and there was a fuzzy, faded green blanket with worn-out letters that said EFFIE. The J had fallen off years ago.

"Jeffrey! You have—a baby blanket?" Robin asked.

"Yup," answered Jeffrey.

"You sleep with it?" asked Robin in amazement. He handed the blanket down.

Jeffrey nodded. "Mom wants me to throw it away. But I can't sleep without it."

"I know what you mean." Robin grinned as he pulled his own blanket out of the knapsack. Jeffrey grinned back at him.

The next morning, Kermit came to pick up Robin.

"How did you sleep?" he asked.

"I slept fine!" said Robin. "Just like a baby!"

Where's Blanket?

Oh, no. Robin lost his blanket. Please help him find it. Trace Robin's walk through the maze. Then you'll find the blanket. Tell what Robin sees along the way.

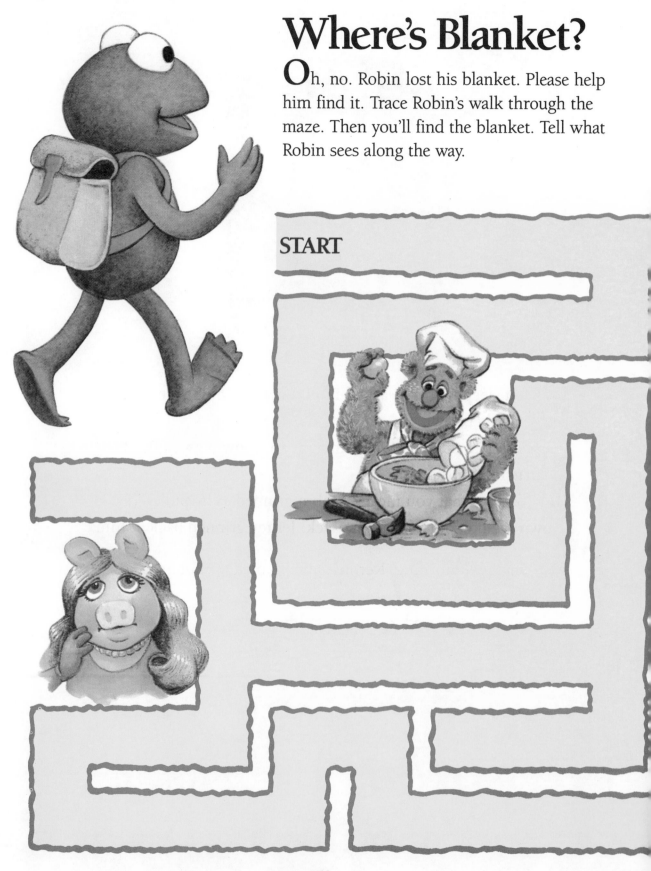

START

FINISH

Fozzie Makes Waves

Fozzie and Kermit stood at the entrance to the park and stared mournfully at the big new white sign.

CLOSED UNTIL THURSDAY, it said. NEW GRASS BEING PLANTED.

"Oh, no!" said Fozzie. "Does this mean we can't have our picnic here?"

By Marianne Meyer

Illustrated by Richard Walz

164

"I guess not," said Kermit. "The park really did need some new grass. Why don't we go to the beach instead?"

Fozzie gulped. "You mean the ocean? Aren't all those waves kind of—well—scary?"

"Scary?" said Kermit. "I don't think so. I really love to jump and splash in the waves. Don't you like to swim?"

Fozzie looked at his feet. "Not really," he said. "Swimming is so . . . wet."

"But you do know how to swim, don't you, Fozzie?" Kermit was concerned.

"Oh, yes," Fozzie said quickly. "Of course I can swim." He looked down again. "I don't care for it very much, that's all."

Kermit found it hard to believe that anyone didn't love to swim. It was one of his very favorite things to do. But he didn't want to upset Fozzie, so he talked about other things on their way to the beach.

"Look Fozzie," he said. "I packed all your favorite foods: peanut-butter-and-banana sandwiches, apples, chocolate milkshakes. . . . "

When they got to the beach, Fozzie wanted to set up the picnic blanket in the parking lot.

"Oh, no," said Kermit. "Let's put it right near the water."

Finally, they agreed to make their picnic at the far end of the sand, away from the ocean.

Kermit wanted to go swimming right away.

"C'mon, Fozzie," he said, heading for the ocean. "I need you to be my swimming buddy. It's not a good idea to go into the water alone."

Fozzie hesitated. "Shouldn't we stay here and make sure the ants don't eat our food?"

"There are no ants," Kermit said. "Let's get wet!"

Kermit raced to the water, and Fozzie followed, but he looked unhappy. He tiptoed into the water and stayed close to the shore. Fozzie didn't appear to be having much fun.

Kermit shrugged. How could anyone not enjoy this wonderful water? He jumped and splashed and swam up and down the shore. He wanted to show off how well he could swim.

"Hey, Fozzie! Watch this!" he yelled, and he did another fancy dive.

Fozzie watched nervously.

"Please be careful," he warned Kermit.

Kermit was so busy diving that he didn't see the big wave coming. The wave swooped up from behind and caught Kermit. It pulled him under.

Fozzie gasped. He couldn't see Kermit. He looked for the lifeguard, but he was busy helping some children who had lost their beach ball. Fozzie took a deep breath and ran through the waves until he found his friend. He was glad he could still touch bottom as he pulled Kermit out of the water.

Fozzie helped Kermit back to their blanket. Kermit coughed a bit, but he was okay.

"Gee, Fozzie," he said. "That wave took me by surprise. I wasn't paying attention."

Fozzie shook like a leaf.

"I'm okay, Fozzie," Kermit said. But Fozzie was still upset.

"Kermit, I don't know how to swim," he confessed. "If the water had been deeper, I couldn't have helped you."

Kermit was confused.

"But you said you *could* swim."

Fozzie looked down sadly. "I was ashamed to tell you I couldn't. Are you angry?"

"Of course not," said Kermit. "Anyway, I was wrong to be showing off. Even frogs have to be careful when they're swimming. You were very brave to run into the deeper water and help me."

"I was?" Fozzie suddenly felt better.

"Sure you were!" Kermit said. "You're a hero! And you know something else? I bet you could learn to swim if you tried. I'd love to teach you."

Fozzie smiled. "I'd like to learn to swim." He paused. "Next time. Right now, I'd like a peanut-butter-and-banana sandwich."

"You've got it, hero!" Kermit exclaimed, and the two sat down for a big, happy picnic.

The Misunderstanding

Rowlf looked at his calendar and his heart sank. Right there, circled in red, was the day of Piggy's big show, her first performance at the town hall. And that day was—yesterday!

Rowlf knew that Piggy had really wanted him to be there. But Rowlf had been busy all day yesterday getting his piano fixed, and he'd forgotten all about the show.

By Kimberly Morris

Illustrated by Richard Walz

"Oh, gosh!" wailed Rowlf, wringing his hands. "Why didn't I look at my calendar yesterday? That way I would have remembered. I'll call Piggy right now and apologize."

Rowlf started to dial the phone, but then he hung up.

"I can't do it," he thought. "I don't know what to say. She'll be mad at me, and I feel so bad already."

Rowlf thought a moment.

"I know what I'll do!" he cried. "I'll write to her and say I'm sorry."

Rowlf ran and got a pen and paper. But when he tried to write his apology, it came out all wrong. There was nothing he could think of to say that would make things all right. Finally, Rowlf gave up.

"I'll think about it tomorrow," he said to himself.

But the next day, Rowlf felt even worse. He decided to wait another day.

So Rowlf waited another day. And another day. And another day. Finally, a whole week had gone by, and he still hadn't called or written to Piggy. The longer he waited, the madder he was afraid she'd be.

By this time, Rowlf was much too embarrassed to see Piggy, so he began to avoid all the places where he might run into her. He stopped going to the grocery store and the coffee shop, and finally he just stayed home.

Then one day, Rowlf got a phone call. It was Smilin' Sam, who had a show on the radio. He wanted to interview Rowlf about songwriting.

Well, Rowlf could hardly say no to that—a chance to be on the radio! So that afternoon, Rowlf went over to the station.

The elevator was waiting in the lobby when he got there. Rowlf got in and pushed the button. But just as the doors began to close, he heard a familiar voice.

"Hold the elevator!" it called. "Wait for *moi*!" In ran Piggy, and the doors closed behind her.

"Piggy!" cried Rowlf. "What are you doing here?"

"I'm going to be interviewed on the radio about my big concert. The concert," Piggy sniffed, "that you didn't come to."

"Oh, Piggy," said Rowlf, "I meant to go. I really did. But . . . well . . . I was busy, and I just forgot about it."

"You forgot!" cried Piggy.

"Yeah. And I'm really, really sorry."

"Then why didn't you call and tell me you forgot?" said Piggy.

"Because I was afraid you'd be mad," said Rowlf, hanging his head.

"Well, you were right," said Piggy. "I *was* mad. But I was even madder when I didn't hear from you. Since you never called, I figured you just didn't care about it. And that really hurt my feelings."

"I'm so sorry, Piggy. I know my apology is late. But will you accept it now?"

Piggy thought a minute. And then she smiled.

"Sure. But next time, don't make it worse by being scared to face me, okay? I might be mad, but I won't bite you."

With that, the elevator doors opened. Smilin' Sam came running over to greet them.

"Well, well!" he said happily. "A songwriter and a singer arriving together. Are you two friends?"

Piggy gave Rowlf a long look. Then she gave him a big hug. "You bet!" she smiled.

"Friends for life!" agreed Rowlf.

The Forget-Me-Not Gallery

Not only does Rowlf play the piano, he's also quite a painter. Some of his paintings are showing at the Forget-Me-Not Gallery. But—oh, dear—Rowlf has forgotten to finish some of the pictures! Look closely at each picture and see if you can find what Rowlf has forgotten to draw.

Home Is Where Your Friends Are

By Harry Ross

Illustrated by Richard Walz

As the curtain fell on the last performance of the Muppet Road Show in the town of Duck's Bend, Fozzie turned sadly to Kermit.

"They don't like me," he said.

"Who doesn't like you?" asked Kermit.

"Them. Out there. The audience," replied Fozzie.

"Of course they like you. They *love* you." Kermit opened the curtain a crack so Fozzie could see them clapping.

"No," Fozzie insisted as they walked back to their dressing rooms. "That spaghetti joke was supposed to be at least a nine and a half on the laugh-o-meter. I bet I only got three and a quarter."

Kermit sat down while Fozzie took off his makeup.

"Well, maybe they don't think spaghetti's funny in Duck's Bend," Kermit said.

"I'll tell you what they don't think is funny in Duck's Bend," said Fozzie. "They don't think Fozzie Bear is funny in Duck's Bend. Just like they didn't think I was funny in Fernsville and Kalamazoo. I tell you, I'm losing my touch."

"What do you think the problem is?" Kermit wanted to know.

"I think I'm homesick. I mean, look at this." Fozzie gestured to the dressing room around him. "Does this look like home?"

Kermit had to admit that it did not.

"We've been on the road too long," said Fozzie. "I miss my home. I miss my stuff. I miss my easy chair and my footstool.

"I miss my library of laughs and my worn old quilt. I even miss the view out my window of the doughnut factory and the smell in the air of fresh-baked doughnuts."

"You're making me hungry," said Kermit. "Let's go eat."

"Okay," said Fozzie, "but the Duck's Bend Diner doesn't serve home-style cooking."

The next day as they were packing up the show train, Kermit gathered Piggy and Gonzo and the others.

"Fozzie's homesick," he said. "Let's come up with something we can do to cheer him up." They put their heads together and did a little thinking.

The next night, as the curtain fell on the first show in the town of Blinker's Nob, Kermit turned to Fozzie and held out a blindfold. "Uhm, mind putting this on, Fozzie?" he said. "It's a surprise."

Fozzie loved surprises. "Sure," he said.

Blindfolded, Fozzie held Kermit's hand as Kermit led him . . . somewhere.

Soon, he began to smell something.

"What's that?" he wondered. "Smells like doughnuts."

"That's right, Fozzie. Because . . ."

Kermit whipped off Fozzie's blindfold.

"This is your home!"

Fozzie looked around his dressing room. There were Piggy and all the others. They had rearranged the furniture to make it look a little like Fozzie's room at home.

"Home!" he said. "Sort of."

"That's right," said Kermit. "There's an easy chair and a footstool, and Piggy sewed some patches onto this old blanket. And we got some joke books at the library. I know it's not much. . . ." Kermit trailed off.

There were tears in Fozzie's eyes.

"You're wrong," Fozzie said. "It's very much, indeed. And I think you've all made me realize something tonight."

"What's that?" Kermit asked.

"You've made me realize that home isn't stuff. Home is friends. And as far as that goes, I'n home all the time with friends like you. Thanks, guys."

"Don't mention it," said Kermit.

"Now, where are those doughnuts?" said Fozzie. "I'm starved."

A Bedtime Punch Line

It was bedtime, but Fozzie just couldn't sleep. Something was bothering him. He couldn't remember the punch line to one of his favorite jokes.

He drank some hot milk, but that didn't work. He tried counting rubber chickens, but that didn't work. Finally, he got out of bed, put on his bathrobe and slippers, and went to Kermit's place. He had to ring the bell three times before Kermit answered the door.

By Richard Chevat

Illustrated by Richard Walz

"Hey, Kermit," said Fozzie, "what did the polar bear say to the grizzly?"

"I don't know," Kermit yawned, rubbing his eyes. "What did the polar bear say to the grizzly?'

"No, no," Fozzie said. "You don't understand. I need *you* to tell me the punch line so I can go to sleep."

"I don't know the punch line, Fozzie."

"Pleeze, Kermit!"

"Okay, okay. How about, 'Let's go to my cave, it's not very fur'?"

"Not very fur?" Fozzie echoed.

"It's not very *fur*," Kermit repeated. "You get it? He said *fur* instead of *far*."

"Oh." Fozzie was very disappointed. "That's not very funny, Kermit," he complained.

"I'm sorry, Fozzie!" Kermit shouted. "That's as funny as I get at two in the morning." And he slammed the door.

After Fozzie had gone, Kermit went back to bed.

"That Fozzie," he said to himself as he snuggled down into his soft green pillow. "Who ever heard of not being able to sleep because of a joke?"

He rolled over and pulled his green blanket over his head.

"What a dumb joke," he thought.

He rolled the other way. Then he opened his eyes wide and sat up in bed.

"I wonder what the polar bear said to the grizzly, anyway?"

Kermit got out of bed, put on his green robe and his green slippers, and started pacing around his bedroom.

"Hmm," he said. "What *did* the polar bear say to the grizzly? How about, 'Have some jam, it's berry good'?"

He thought for a moment. "No, that's not funny.

"How about, 'I can't go on; I have two paws'?"

Kermit shook his head again. "No, that's not funny.

"I know!" he said after a few minutes. "The polar bear didn't say much because he had a short tail!"

"No," he moaned. "That can't be it. I can't stand it!" he cried. "Now *I* can't sleep! I'm going to see Fozzie."

So Kermit headed for Fozzie's house. On his way, he met Miss Piggy, Gonzo, Scooter, and Rowlf, all dressed in their pajamas and bathrobes.

"Did Fozzie wake you up also?" he asked. They all nodded.

"Yes, and not one of us has been able to sleep because of that dumb joke," Piggy said.

"Well, I'm going to find out the answer," Kermit said, and he led them into Fozzie's house.

There was Fozzie, fast asleep, snoring.

"Fozzie," they said, shaking the sleeping bear. "You have to *think*. What did the polar bear say to the grizzly?"

Fozzie snorted and rolled over.

"Go to sleep, everyone," he mumbled, without opening his eyes. Then he started snoring again.

"'Go to sleep, everyone'?" Piggy said. "What kind of punch line is that?"

"I don't think it's very funny," added Scooter.

"Me, neither," said Rowlf.

"Well," said Kermit, "it may not be a good punch line, but it's good advice. Go to sleep, everyone."

And that's exactly what they did.

Rowlf's Lullaby

"Yaaaaawwwwn! I'm going to sleep," said Rowlf, as he marched off to his bedroom. Today had been a very busy day. "And tomorrow," thought Rowlf, "is going to be even busier. I promised Kermit I'd write a go-to-sleep song. If I don't get some rest, I'll never think of the right notes."

By Jim Lewis

Illustrated by Richard Walz

Rowlf's bed was warm and cozy, with a big puffy pillow and soft fluffy blankets. He settled himself between the covers, gave one more great big yawn, and was off to . . .

PLINK! PLINK! PLINK!
"What?" said Rowlf, sitting up in bed.
It was just the faucet dripping in the sink. "I'll fix that tomorrow," thought Rowlf, "just as soon as I write Kermit's go-to-sleep song. Right now, I'm going to sleep."
Rowlf closed his eyes, put his head on the pillow, and was off to . . .

WHOOO! WHOOO! BONK!
WHOOO! WHOOO! BONK!
"Huh?" said Rowlf, raising himself up on his paws.
It was just the window shutters blowing in the breeze.
"I'll tie those down tomorrow," thought Rowlf, "just as soon as I write Kermit's go-to-sleep song and fix the dripping faucet. But now, I'm going to sleep."
So Rowlf shut his eyes and was quickly off to. . .

YIP! YIP! AH-ROOO!
YIP! YIP! AH-ROOO!
"What's that?!" exclaimed Rowlf, rushing to the window. It was just Rowlf's cousins, Bow and Wow Barkington, out in the alley singing a dog song. Rowlf liked their song, but not so late at night.
"Tomorrow I will ask them not to sing so loud," thought Rowlf, "just as soon as I write Kermit's go-to-sleep song, fix the dripping faucet and tie down the shutters. But right now, I'm going to sleep."

So Rowlf climbed back into bed, pulled up the covers and was almost sound asleep. . .

WEEEE! GEEEE! WEEEE!
GEEEE! WEEEE! GEEEE!
"Who's making that noise?" said
Rowlf, tossing off his covers.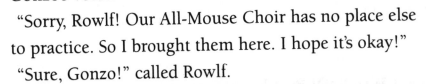
From downstairs Rowlf heard
Gonzo's voice.
"Sorry, Rowlf! Our All-Mouse Choir has no place else to practice. So I brought them here. I hope it's okay!"
"Sure, Gonzo!" called Rowlf.

"I'll give Gonzo and his All-Mouse Choir a key to my music room," thought Rowlf, "just as soon as I write Kermit's go-to-sleep song, fix the dripping faucet, tie down the shutters, and remind Bow and Wow Barkington not to sing so loud so late at night."

By now it was very late and Rowlf was very tired. But he couldn't fall asleep. He lay in bed and stared at the ceiling.
"Oh, dear," he thought. "If I don't get to sleep, I'll never think of the right notes for Kermit's go-to-sleep song. Which means that I won't". . .
PLINK! PLINK!
"fix the dripping faucet" . . .
WHOOO! WHOOO! BONK! . . .
"tie down the shutters " . . .
YIP! YIP! AH-ROO! . . .
"talk to Bow and Wow Barkington about not singing so loud or". . .

WEEEE! GEEEE! WEEEE! GEEEE! . . .

"give Gonzo and his All-Mouse Choir the key to my music room."

Now, as everyone knows, some of our best ideas come when we're about to fall asleep. And sure enough, just as he was drifting off, Rowlf had one of his best ideas ever.

"I'll make all those noises into music!" he said. And Rowlf began to sing, to the tune of Brahms' famous lullaby:

"WHOOO! WHOOO! BONK!
WHOOO! WHOOO! BONK!
PLINK! PLINK! PLINK! PLINK! PLINK! PLINK! PLINK!
WEEEE! GEEEE! YIP!
WEEEE! GEEEE! YIP!
AH-ROO! AH-ROO!
WHOOO! WHOOO! BONK! . . ."

It was a perfectly wonderful go-to-sleep song. It was so wonderful, in fact, that Rowlf fell asleep at the last BONK.

And there he is, sound asleep in his warm, cozy bed. Shhh! He needs his rest. Tomorrow is going to be a very, very busy day.

Kermit's Lullaby

"Settle down, Robin," Kermit said. "It's time to go to sleep."

"But, Uncle Kermit," Robin answered, sitting up in bed, "I don't feel sleepy at all!"

"Try counting salamanders," Kermit said, sitting down beside Robin.

By Richard Chevat   *Illustrated by Richard Walz*

"I tried that," Robin complained. "It didn't work."

"Well, what might work?" Kermit wanted to know.

"Sing me a lullaby," Robin answered.

"Okay," Kermit said. "But just one. And then, off to sleep! Now, lie down and close your eyes."

"Yes, Uncle Kermit," said Robin, and Kermit began to sing softly:

> *"Hush, little tadpole,*
> *don't make a croak,*
> *Momma's gonna . . ."*

"That's not how it goes," said Robin. "It's 'Hush, little baby, don't say a word.'"

"This is the frog version," said Kermit. "Now, listen." And he began again:

> *"Hush, little tadpole, don't make a croak,*
> *Momma's gonna buy you a place to soak.*
> *And if that place to soak springs a leak,*
> *Momma's gonna buy you a house in the creek."*

"In the creek?" Robin said, sitting up. He tried to imagine what a house in a creek looked like. "Why does he want a house in a creek?"

"Because tadpoles like creeks!" Kermit replied. "Now, hush!"

"Okay," said Robin. "But it sounds funny."

"Lie down!" said Kermit, and he started singing once more:

> *"And if that house in the creek should break,*
> *Momma's gonna buy you a muddy lake.*
> *And if that muddy lake goes dry . . ."*

"Uncle Kermit?" Robin interrupted.

"Yes?" said Kermit.

"Why does the lake go dry?"

"Why?" Kermit sighed. "Just because!"

"Oh," Robin said.

"Where was I?" Kermit asked.

"The lake went dry," answered Robin.

"Oh, yeah," said Kermit. And he sang:

> *"And if that muddy lake goes dry,*
> *Momma's gonna buy you a dragonfly.*
> *And if that dragonfly . . ."*

"Uncle Kermit?"

"Yes?" groaned Kermit.

"Why do they call it a dragonfly?"

"Why, why, why?" Kermit cried. "Because! Now, don't ask me why anymore!"

"Why?" asked Robin.

"Robin, do you want me to sing this song or not?" Kermit asked.

"Yes, please, Uncle Kermit," said Robin.

"Then please don't interrupt me anymore!" Kermit begged.

And he started the song all over again from the beginning:

> *"Hush, little tadpole, don't make a croak,*
> *Momma's gonna buy you a place to soak.*
> *And if that place to soak springs a leak,*
> *Momma's gonna buy you a house in the creek.*
> *And if that house in the creek should break,*
> *Momma's gonna buy you a muddy lake.*
> *And if that muddy lake goes dry,*

Momma's gonna buy you a dragonfly.
And if that dragonfly is bad,
Momma's gonna buy you a lily pad.
And if that lily pad gets soggy,
Momma's gonna buy you a swamp that's boggy.
And if that swamp stops being a bog,
Momma's gonna buy you a hollow log.
And if that log turns upside down,
you'll still be the cutest little tadpole around."

Kermit sang the whole song, and when he was done, Robin didn't say a thing. His head was on the pillow and his eyes were closed.

"Asleep at last," Kermit said softly.

He stood up and began to tiptoe out of the room.

Just as he reached the door, he heard a little frog voice. It was Robin's.

"That was nice, Uncle Kermit," he said. "Sing it again."

"Oh, why?" Kermit sighed.

"Because," mumbled Robin, and then he nodded off to sleep.

Sweet Dreams

Here's a nice lullaby to sing at bedtime with someone you love. Point to each picture on the right as you sing along.

Rock-a-bye

In the 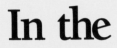 top.

When the wind blows,

The  will rock.

When the bough breaks,

The  will fall.

And down will come

 and all.

Baby Gonzo Gets His Wish

By Ellen Weiss

Illustrated by Tom Cooke

"Hey, look at this!" exclaimed Gonzo. He'd been banging and clanking around the very back of the kitchen closet, while Nanny washed the dishes from lunch.

"What did you find, Gonzo?" asked Nanny.

"I don't know, but it's neat," said Gonzo. "I think it might be a gold nose-cover."

Nanny turned to look, and then she laughed.

"Oh, that's an old brass lamp," she said. "It's been in the back of the closet for so long, it's all tarnished. Would you like to polish it?"

"Sure!" said Gonzo.

So Nanny gave him some polish and a cloth, and he sat down in a corner and started to work. He rubbed and he rubbed, and the lamp got shinier and shinier. And as he rubbed, he began to daydream.

Suddenly, a wisp of blue smoke began snaking out of the lamp—and then a whole cloud of smoke. And out of the smoke stepped a strange-looking fellow with a large mustache.

"I am the genie of the lamp," announced the fellow. "Thank you for letting me out. What are your three wishes?"

"You mean, I can just wish for something and you'll arrange it?" asked Gonzo in amazement.

"Your wish is my command," said the genie.

"Okay," said Gonzo, thinking hard. "This is great! I'll have all the marshmallows in the world, please."

The genie nodded. All at once, Gonzo heard a loud roaring sound and began to smell the sweet smell of marshmallows in the air. And then they started coming . . . millions of marshmallows . . . billions of marshmallows . . . pouring in the windows . . . knocking down the doors . . . even coming out of the kitchen faucet. They filled up the kitchen, piling up higher and higher, until they were up to Gonzo's nose. In a minute, he was going to be covered in marshmallows!

"Wait!" yelled Gonzo, his voice muffled by marshmallows. "Hold on! Cancel that wish! Forget it! Ixnay on the wish!"

"Your wish is my command," said the genie, and the marshmallows disappeared.

"Whew! That was close!" gasped Gonzo. "I'll have to be more careful with the next wish."

Gonzo began thinking. He thought and he thought, until the genie began to tap his foot. But at last, Gonzo had it.

"I wish I could fly," he said.

"No problem," said the genie.

Gonzo gave his arms a little test flap, just to see what would happen. He rose into the air about a foot. Flapping harder, he shot up into the air and bumped into the kitchen ceiling.

"Ow!" he said. He rubbed his head, flapped his arms sideways, and sailed straight through the kitchen window.

Unfortunately, he'd forgotten about the sycamore tree that was just outside the window.

"Ooch!" he said, rubbing his nose where it had hit the tree. He flew back into the kitchen.

Gonzo's arms were getting very tired. "I think it's time to take a rest," said Gonzo to himself, flapping toward the floor. But, as hard as he tried, he couldn't seem to land. He just floated about in the middle of the room.

"Hey, Mr. Genie!" called Gonzo. "Why can't I land?"

"You didn't wish anything about landing," said the genie. "Only flying."

"Let me down, you meanie-genie!" said Gonzo.

"Okay, I'll do you a favor. But just this once," said the genie. He let Gonzo down with a loud thump.

"I wish you were never in that lamp!" cried Gonzo, rubbing his knee.

And in that instant, Gonzo wasn't rubbing his knee anymore. He was rubbing the lamp.

"Good job!" said Nanny. "It's nice and shiny."

Gonzo peered inside the lamp. "And it's nice and empty, too," he added. "Thank goodness."

Babes in Snowland

It was way past Halloween, a little bit after Thanksgiving, and getting close to Christmas, and still there was no snow. However, throughout the nursery, the Babies were thinking winter thoughts—thoughts of glistening icicles, sleighs, and snowdrifts.

By Charles Hirsch   *Illustrated by Tom Cooke*

"Oh, I want it to snow," sighed Baby Piggy as she began to shake up the snowflakes in her glass paperweight.

"Oh, we want it to snow," chimed in the Babies as they watched the pretend snow swirl around the figure of the snowman inside the paperweight.

As Piggy twirled and the snow swirled, the Babies suddenly found themselves in Snowland, a place where everything, including trees and houses and horses' saddles, was made of snow.

"There's Mr. Snowman," said Piggy, pointing to a sad-looking fellow sitting on a cloud of snow next to his snow machine.

"Oh, Mr. Snowman, why didn't you make any snow this year?" the Babies asked.

"Oh, I don't know," said Mr. Snowman. "I'm tired of the snow. It's just so white. It isn't blue, like the sky. And it's not green, like the grass. And it's not purple and red, like my favorite sweater. It's just white. It's all the same."

And then he added, "Besides, it's too cold and wet."

"But don't forget how wonderful the snow is," said Piggy as she took some paper from her purse. With a snip, snip, snip, she cut out a snowflake that looked as delicate and beautiful as the lace around the tops of her socks.

"Every single snowflake is different," she reminded Mr. Snowman.

"You're right," admitted Mr. Snowman, "but the snow's still too cold and wet."

"No, it isn't," said Baby Kermit. And quick as a wink, he lay flat on his back in the snow.

After a *swish . . . swish . . . swish* of his arms and legs, up and down and back and forth, he jumped back up. The image of an angel was pressed in the snowbank.

"Well, I guess the snow's not too cold and wet to play in," remarked Mr. Snowman. "But, I'm still bored with it."

In what seemed faster than a flurry, the Babies took their thoughts of icicles, their winter dreams, and their wishes for snow and threw them into the snow machine.

The snow machine lugged.

Then it chugged.

Then it laughed.

And it began to throw out snow. Snow that was silvery white and bluish white and all sorts of colorful whites.

And the Babies screamed and hollered and laughed and played. They were so happy with all the snow.

Mr. Snowman watched the Babies playing in the snow, and he began to remember all the wonderful winters he had seen in his lifetime.

"Let it snow!" he declared, throwing his own memories into the machine.

More and more snow began to twirl and swirl.

The Babies closed their eyes and whirled around and around and around. . . .

When they opened their eyes, they were back in the nursery.

"Look, everybody," said Nanny. "It's snowing."

"Yippee," sang the Babies as they dashed to put on their coats and hats and galoshes.

They were on their way outdoors to play in the very first snowfall of winter.

Baby Kermit's Safari

One day in the nursery, Baby Kermit climbed into his little blue jeep. "I think I'll go on safari in Africa today," he decided. "Safaris are always fun."

Kermit stared straight ahead and said to himself, "Africa. Africa."

By Deborah Kovacs

Illustrated by Tom Cooke

At first, all he saw were the nursery walls. But he kept thinking about going to Africa, and soon the jeep's wheels began to turn.

Kermit began drifting away to a misty place.

Suddenly, he heard a loud noise.

"*Ai-eee!*" it went.

"What's that?" said Kermit.

He looked around and saw that he was in a clearing in the jungle. Nearby, he saw a little elephant running in circles, very upset, sticking her trunk in the air and trumpeting "*Ai-eeeeee!*"

Kermit drove over to the elephant.

"What's wrong?" he asked.

"My mommy! My mommy! She's lost!" cried the elephant.

A parrot flapped next to the elephant's head.

"Now, now, Annabelle," clucked the parrot, "your mother's not lost. We are."

Kermit looked puzzled, so the parrot explained:

"Eloise, the mother elephant, asked me to watch Annabelle for a little while. We decided to take a walk, and now we can't find our way back to where we're supposed to meet Eloise."

"Climb into my jeep," said Kermit. "We'll find her."

"Gosh, thanks!" said Annabelle as she climbed aboard, tipping Kermit's jeep sideways a little. The parrot perched on top of the elephant's head, and they were off.

"Which way?" said Kermit.

Annabelle pointed with her trunk. "Let's go this way," she said.

They drove down the jungle path to Gorilla Gorge, and pretty soon they saw a gorilla. He was dangling from a tall tree, eating a banana.

"Have you seen my mother?" asked Annabelle anxiously.

The gorilla scratched his head. "Big gray animal, baggy knees, looking for her child?" he said.

"That's my mom!" said the baby elephant excitedly.

"She went that way," said the gorilla, pointing with his banana.

They headed down the path again, this time to Zebra Hollow. They didn't see Eloise, but they did see a zebra.

"Have you seen this elephant's mother?" said Kermit.

"Yes, I have," said the zebra. "She said she was going to look for her baby at the water hole."

"Where's the water hole?" asked Kermit.

"It's that way," said the zebra, pointing with his nose.

So off they went, to the water hole. And who should they find there, but the little elephant's mother!

"*Ai-eeeee!*" trumpeted Eloise.

"*Ai-eeeee!*" trumpeted Annabelle. They hugged each other with their trunks, happy to be together once more.

Then Eloise turned to the parrot.

"Why did you wander away?" she asked sternly. "You were supposed to stay put."

"I'm sorry," said the parrot, hanging his head. "I thought we'd come right back."

The mother elephant sighed through her trunk. "Please don't ever do that again," she said. But then she smiled and said, "Well, anyway, we found each other!"

She turned to Baby Kermit

"Thanks for helping us, little frog."

Kermit smiled. "No problem. Just think of me as an elephant's best friend."

"We'll never forget you!" said both the elephants.

Kermit waved and climbed into his jeep. He was feeling a little hungry; it was time to go home.

"Nursery. Nursery," he said to himself, and in the twinkle of an eye, his little blue jeep was right back where it had started.

"Kermit, you're just in time for a snack!" said Fozzie.

"What are we having?"
asked Kermit.

"Animal crackers," said Fozzie.

"I saved an elephant for you."

"That's funny," Kermit replied.

"I saved an elephant, too."

And he smiled.

Safari Search

Baby Kermit is looking for his animal friends in the jungle. See if you can spot them all. Look for:

1 crocodile slithering along

2 hippos resting in the water

3 fluttering butterflies

4 birds way up high

Baby Fozzie's Green Thumb

Baby Fozzie was reading the new bestselling book, *You Too Can Have a Green Thumb*. He knew he had a golden funny bone, but he wasn't so sure about having a green thumb. So to find out, he decided to grow something right in the nursery windowbox.

By Harry Ross

Illustrated by Tom Cooke

The next sunny morning, Fozzie dug a little hole in the dirt.

He planted some tomato seeds. He covered them gently. He watered them. Then he pulled up a chair and sat down to wait.

Two days passed, but no tomato plant sprouted. Fozzie sighed and shook his head.

"I wonder what I'm doing wrong."

Kermit overheard him.

"Why don't you try talking to your plants?" Kermit said. "It may sound weird, but I hear it works."

"I've never talked to a plant before," Fozzie replied. "What do I say?"

"I don't know. Why not do what you do best? Tell it a joke," Kermit suggested.

So Fozzie said to the dirt, "What did the garden say to the farmer? Hoe, hoe, hoe! Get it?"

Two days later, Fozzie had told every joke he knew—and some of them twice.

"Why are you always talking to the windowbox, Fozzie?" Piggy asked.

"Kermit said talking to plants helps them grow," declared Fozzie.

"Silly," said Piggy. "Everybody knows that plants don't grow unless you feed them."

"Feed them what?" Fozzie asked.

"How should I know?" Piggy replied. "What would you like if you were a cute little tomato plant?"

Fozzie scratched his head and thought until he came up with the perfect menu. He fixed his plant spinach, so it would grow big and strong; and watermelon ice cream, so it would feel in the pink; and potato chips, so it would grow up to be crisp and snappy.

He put everything on a plate, set the plate on the edge of the windowbox, and sat back to wait. Two days later, the spinach had wilted, the ice cream had melted, and the chips were mighty soggy.

"I hear you're growing something," said Gonzo.

"Yes," said Fozzie. "I'm growing very discouraged. I've been waiting for days and days, and there's still no tomato."

"What you need is a scarecrow," Gonzo told him. "Every good garden has one."

So Fozzie proceeded to make a scarecrow by stuffing newspapers into an old shirt and a raggedy pair of pants.

After the scarecrow was set up and watching over his garden, Fozzie decided he could go and do something else for a change.

First he played chopsticks with Rowlf on the toy piano.

Then Piggy invited him to have a tea party with her dolls.

The next day, he built a gigantic tower of blocks with Scooter. He was just putting the finishing touches on the tower when Piggy came running.

"Fozzie! Fozzie!" she called. "You'll never believe what happened!"

"What?" he asked, scratching his head.

"Do you remember that cute little tomato plant that wasn't growing?"

"Oh!" Fozzie jumped up. In fact, he had been so busy for the past day and a half, he had completely forgotten about his garden.

He ran to the windowbox. Sure enough, there it was: the cutest, greenest little tomato plant he had ever seen.

"I guess all that hard work and good advice paid off," said Fozzie, smiling happily.

"And I guess I forgot to tell you the most important thing of all," Kermit said. "It's about patience. All growing things take time."

"Yes," Fozzie said, looking fondly down at his plant. "But it was worth every minute."

The Wide
World
Of Gonzo

By Kimberly Morris

Illustrated by Tom Cooke

"*Ah-choo! Ah-choo!*" sneezed Gonzo.

"That sounds like a cold," said Nanny, handing him a tissue. "I'm afraid that means a day in bed."

"But I don't want to stay in bed all day," snuffled Gonzo. "It's boring."

"It doesn't have to be," said Nanny. "Here! You can look through this adventure magazine."

"Oh, Nanny," grumbled Gonzo. "I don't want to look at pictures of other people's adventures when I can't have any myself."

Nanny smiled and went to the cupboard. She took out the paste and the safety scissors and some photographs of Gonzo.

"Why don't you cut up these snapshots, and then paste the pictures of yourself into the magazine?" she said. "Then you can pretend it's you in the magazine having the adventures."

Gonzo sighed unhappily as Nanny left the room.

But then he smiled when he opened the magazine and saw a picture of a cowboy riding a big white horse.

"Boy!" said Gonzo. "Wouldn't I love to be that cowboy!"

So he pasted a picture of himself over the picture of the cowboy. And when he'd finished, it really did look like it was Gonzo on the back of the horse.

He was just about to turn the page when, suddenly, his bed began to lurch and bounce. It startled Gonzo so much that his arms flew up in the air. When he looked up, he saw that his hand wasn't holding a magazine anymore. It was holding a ten-gallon cowboy hat! When he looked down, he saw that he was on the back of a real live horse—and it was bucking!

Gonzo pushed the hat down on his head and hung on to the saddle. The horse was bouncing and lurching, and Gonzo was loving every minute of it. It was better than a roller coaster. He hoped the ride would go on and on and on.

But then the horse gave a final bounce, and Cowboy Gonzo went flying out of the saddle. He squeezed his eyes shut, expecting to land on the hard and dusty ground. But instead, he landed with a nice, soft thump, right back in his own bed.

"That was great," he said. "Now, what next?"

He flipped through the magazine until he found a picture of some people parachuting out of a plane.

As soon as he'd pasted a picture of himself beneath one of the parachutes, his bed began swaying gently back and forth. He looked up and saw that he was dangling from a red silk parachute. It gave him a delicious and mysterious feeling in his tummy.

And when his feet finally touched the ground, the huge parachute collapsed around him like a big silk tent.

Gonzo peeked out from beneath the parachute and discovered that, once again, he was back in his own bed. He peered out from under the quilt into Kermit's curious face.
"Gee, Gonzo," said Kermit. "What are you doing?"
"Oh, Kermit!" exclaimed Gonzo."I've been having the most wonderful adventures!"
"Gosh!" said Kermit. "And I thought you were just having a cold."

Doubting Thomas

One day, Lolly Polliwog was swimming close to the shore of Swampy Pond. As she swam, she sang a little song that went like this:

"There's a little bit of magic—
I can feel it in the air.
There's a little bit of magic
All around me everywhere!"

By Michaela Muntean

Illustrated by John Gurney

Thomas Polliwog, who was swimming nearby, heard her.

"That's the silliest song I've ever heard," he said. "What do you mean about magic being everywhere? I don't see any magic around here."

"Of course there's magic," said Lolly. "Swim a little closer to shore with me and poke your head out of the water. Now, look at the web that spider has spun between those two flowers. Don't you think that's magical?"

"Spiders are always building webs," said Thomas. "There's nothing magical about that."

"Well," said Lolly, "what about that acorn on the ground? It will grow into a big oak tree, you know."

"It will?" said Thomas, who had to admit that he hadn't known that. "If we wait here, can we watch it happen?"

"Oh, no," laughed Lolly. "It takes a long time for a tree to grow."

"I knew it!" said Thomas. "I knew it couldn't be magic. There's nothing magical about a tree growing."

"Well," said Lolly, "I'll give you another example. Do you see that caterpillar crawling up the stem of that daisy? Sometime soon it will be a butterfly."

Thomas stared at the caterpillar. "Do you mean that that long, fuzzy, funny-looking thing will someday turn into a beautiful butterfly?"

"Yes," said Lolly. "And I'll tell you something else—soon *we* will turn into frogs."

"I'll say one thing for you," Thomas said. "You sure have some imagination! How could little polliwogs like us turn into big frogs?"

"Just wait and see," said Lolly.

So Thomas waited, and while he waited, he came to visit Lolly every day. And every day, she talked to him about the magical things that were all around them.

She told him that there was a little bit of magic in how a rainbow would sometimes appear in the sky after a rain. And she told him that there must be a little bit of magic in how flowers could grow from such tiny seeds.

And every day, things were beginning to happen to Lolly and Thomas.

Their back legs were growing longer and stronger.

Then their front legs began to grow.

Their heads grew bigger and their tails grew smaller.

One day, Lolly and Thomas were no longer polliwogs. They were little frogs that could hop out of the pond whenever they wanted and then hop back in for a swim.

One day, while they were sunning themselves on the shore, Thomas said, "You know, Lolly, I didn't believe you when you told me that someday we would be frogs."

"I know you didn't," Lolly answered. "You had to see it happen for yourself."

"But now I understand what you mean about magic," Thomas said. "About the magic in an acorn, and a spider's web, and a rainbow, and—in us."

Lolly smiled and began to sing. This time, Thomas joined in.
"There's a little bit of magic—
We can feel it in the air.
There's a little bit of magic
All around us everywhere!"

Baby Kermit's
Magic Blanket Ride

Kermit's blanket was his favorite thing in the world. It was
small, soft, and yellow, and it had a wonderful smell. He took
his blanket with him everywhere and slept with it every night.
To Kermit, this blanket was a toy, a costume, and a very special
friend, all rolled into one.

By Deborah Kovacs   *Illustrated by Tom Cooke*

"Kermie," said Piggy one morning, "why don't you put your blanket away and come and play with us? We're going to play hide-and-seek."

"I don't know," said Kermit dreamily. "Maybe a little later."

He took his blanket over to a corner of the room and laid it out flat on the floor.

"You and I can have a lot of fun together, blanket," said Kermit, gently patting it. Soon, he felt himself and his blanket drifting together to a misty land. . . .

Slowly, the blanket rose from the nursery floor. It floated in the air. Kermit sat cozily in the middle of it and looked over its edges. He could see the others, still playing on the nursery floor.

"Take me someplace really different today, blanket," said Kermit.

The blanket lifted Kermit a little higher in the air, to an open window. Together, they floated out the window and hovered over the neighborhood.

"I wonder where we're going," said Kermit to himself.

The blanket rose in the sky. Higher and higher it went. Below them, Kermit could see the people and cars on the streets growing smaller and smaller. Soon he could only see buildings. And then even the buildings were too small to see.

"Are we going to the moon?" he asked the blanket, wonderingly.

As if in answer, the blanket rose higher still. The sky was dark all around them, except for the twinkling of distant stars. They were in outer space! Kermit was wearing a space helmet and a space suit, with gloves. He peered back over his shoulder. There was the Earth, looking like an enormous white, green, brown, and blue marble in the sky, growing farther and farther away.

"Blanket, this is the greatest ride ever!" said Kermit.

They were getting very close to the moon. It loomed before them, huge and glowing white, in the dark sky.

"Can we land there for a while?" asked Kermit, breathless with excitement.

Just over the moon's surface, the blanket slowed down. It landed with a thump, which gave Kermit a jolt.

"That was one small thump for a blanket," said Kermit, "but one giant bump for a frog!" He got up and took a few steps.

The surface of the moon felt grainy and crunchy. Kermit's body felt so light, he found that he could jump high into the air with almost no effort at all. He *boinged* around happily for quite a long time. Then he hopped up to a small pile of moon rocks. He picked one up and stuck it inside one of his space gloves. It had a rough surface, full of holes.

It was wonderful being on the moon. But there was one thing missing.

"I'm hungry," said Kermit. "And we didn't bring any food with us. We'd better go back to the nursery."

Kermit got back on the blanket.

"Home, blanket," he said.

Smoothly, the blanket rose again. Together, they sped through the blackness of space.

Kermit felt the space suit slip off as they got back to Earth.

Before long, they flew over Kermit's house and right up to the nursery window, which was still open. They floated in and landed with a thud on the rug.

"Lunchtime," called Nanny.

"Come on, Kermit," said Piggy. "You missed all the fun."

Kermit looked down at his wonderful blanket. "That's what you think!" he said softly, as he joined his friends for lunch.

Baby Skeeter Sets a Record

By Kimberly Morris

Illustrated by Tom Cooke

One morning at breakfast, Baby Skeeter made an announcement.

"I have decided," she said, "to set a record."

"Gosh," said Kermit, "what does that mean?"

"Setting a record means doing something better or longer or more times than anybody else. For instance, if I sat on a flagpole for more hours than anybody else, I'd set the record for flagpole sitting. See?"

"That sounds neat," said Kermit. "But what are you going to set a record for?"

"I don't know yet," said Skeeter. "All I know is that I'm determined to set a record for something."

When Nanny set down a platter of her delicious pancakes, Skeeter shouted, "I know! I'll set a record for eating the most pancakes."

So Skeeter proceeded to eat pancake after pancake. After about the twelfth one, her tummy began to feel very peculiar. In fact, she felt just awful and had to go lie down.

"At this rate," she groaned, "I'll never set a record."

But after a little nap, Skeeter felt well enough to join in a game of hide-and-seek.

She hid herself under all the towels in the laundry hamper and whispered to herself happily, "I know. I'll stay in here for two weeks and set a record for hide-and-seek."

But as the minutes ticked by, two weeks began to seem like an awfully long time. "This is too boring," said Skeeter.

So she climbed out of the hamper, went back into the nursery, and found an old pair of stilts. "Now, *this* is just the thing. I'll set a record for spending the most time on stilts."

Skeeter spent the rest of the day walking around on her stilts. By dinnertime, she felt so comfortable on her stilts that she offered to race Kermit to the end of the nursery.

As they sped along, Skeeter was so excited that she didn't see the big red ball sitting on the floor, right in her path.

Crash! She tripped and fell off her stilts and onto her bottom.

"Skeeter! Are you all right?" asked Kermit.

"Sure," said Skeeter bravely. But she really wasn't. Actually, she was very frustrated and very embarrassed. As she picked herself up, a tear trickled down her cheek.

That night after dinner, Kermit tapped on his water glass with a spoon.

"Ahem. May I have your attention, please?" he said. "Nanny told me that today is April third. So from now on, April third will be remembered as the day that Skeeter set a record."

"But I didn't," cried Skeeter, "even though I tried really hard!"

"That's just it," said Rowlf. "And nobody else we know has ever tried as hard as you. So that means you set the record for trying the hardest to set a record!"

"Set record! Set record!" yelled Animal.

"Thanks, everybody!" said Skeeter happily. "But you know what I *really* set the record for?"

"What?" yelled Animal.

"It's the record," grinned Skeeter, "for having the best bunch of friends in the whole world."

The Thingdo

A very exciting letter had just been delivered to the nursery. "Congratulations!" the letter said. "You have won a FREE THINGDO! It will be delivered to your address very soon."

By Kimberly Morris

Illustrated by Tom Cooke

"Isn't that wonderful!" sang Baby Piggy.

"Lucky us!" shouted Baby Kermit.

"Yippee!" cried Baby Rowlf as he grabbed Baby Fozzie by the arms and danced him around the nursery. "Isn't that great!"

But Fozzie looked a little bewildered.

"I think so," he said, "but what exactly *is* a Thingdo?"

"It's something to eat," said Kermit, "isn't it?"

"I thought it was something to play with," said Piggy.

"I thought it was something to ride on," said Rowlf.

Just then, Scooter came running into the nursery with a brown paper package.

"It's here!" he shouted.

They all gathered around as he tore away the paper and opened the box.

"Ohhhhh," they all sighed in disappointment. "It's nothing but a rock."

"Gee," said Rowlf. "I was really hoping it was something to ride on."

All of a sudden, the sound of an engine came roaring up out of the box. Before their very eyes, the rock changed into a rocket ship.

"Go, go, go!" cried Animal.

229

All the Babies jumped inside the rocket ship. Rockets flared out behind them, and they zoomed out the window, going about a million miles an hour.

Soon they were orbiting Mars, zigzagging between meteors, and doing figure eights around the Moon.

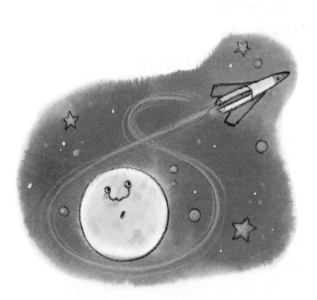

Then they plunged hundreds of thousands of miles back to Earth, coming to a breathless stop back at the nursery.

Whew! They all agreed that it had been the most exciting ride they had ever been on.

"That was fun," said Piggy, "but I was really hoping for something to play with."

And as soon as the words were out of her mouth—*presto!*— the Thingdo turned into the oddest-looking ball any of them had ever seen. It was sort of every shape and no shape at all—kind of roundish-squarish, biggish-smallish, and longish-shortish.

And what a wonderful ball it was! Sometimes it bounced up in the air. Sometimes it dribbled around in circles. Sometimes it flew away and came right back like a boomerang.

After an hour or so of playing odd-ball with their very odd
ball, the Babies were very, very hungry.

"Boy," said Kermit, twirling the ball on the tip of his finger,
"wouldn't it be nice to have something good to eat right now?"

With that, the ball flew straight up in the air, spun around,
turned into a pie, and came back down, landing right in the
middle of the nursery table.

Everybody had a piece. And it was so delicious, they finished
every last crumb.

The only problem was—now the Thingdo was gone. Actually,
that was all right with the Babies. They had had enough
excitement for one day.

Maybe next time, *you'll* win the Thingdo.

The Team Spirit

"Leapfrog, everybody!" Kermit sang out. "Time to play leapfrog!"

Everybody in the nursery was excited. Everybody, that is, except Scooter.

By Harry Ross

Illustrated by Tom Cooke

"I don't want to play," he called from where he sat at his computer. "I'm no good at jumping over people. I'm not the athletic type."

"But we need you!" said his sister, Skeeter.

"I'll only be in the way," protested Scooter. "I'm sorry, but I'm not playing."

And so Scooter sat and watched as everyone else laughed and yelled and played leapfrog. He wasn't really looking at his computer at all—he was looking at his friends having fun.

At story time that night, Scooter didn't really listen to the fairy tale Nanny read.

At bath time, he didn't even play with his boat.

And when it was time to go to sleep, he just lay there, staring at the ceiling. Why was he so afraid to try playing leapfrog? he wondered sadly. At last he drifted off to sleep.

It seemed he had been asleep only a very short time when a figure—who reminded him strangely of Skeeter—appeared at the foot of the crib.

"Behold, Scooter," said the figure. "I am the Team Spirit."

Scooter sat up and rubbed his eyes. "What do you want?"

"I want you to play leapfrog!" said the Team Spirit.

"But I can't," said Scooter. "I'm just not the athletic type."

"You could learn," said the Spirit.

"But I'm hopeless at games," said Scooter.

"You're good at computer games, aren't you?" said the Spirit.

"But I'm scared of jumping. I might get hurt."

"And you might not. You'll never know unless you try," said the Spirit. "And not trying is one of the saddest things of all."

"I might trip and look silly," said Scooter.

"Everybody trips and looks silly now and then. You might look silly, it's true. But then again, you might look great. Find your own special strength. Everybody has a strength— even you."

"I doubt it," said Scooter.

"Here," said the Spirit. "Try playing some leapfrog with me."

As she pointed her finger at Scooter, he felt himself rising magically out of the crib.

And before he knew it, he was playing a great game of leapfrog with the Team Spirit.

"Not bad," said the Spirit. "Will we see you in the game tomorrow?"

"I think so," said Scooter shyly.

"What was that?" asked the Spirit.

"Yes!" said Scooter. "I like leapfrog. I will play!"

"That's the old team spirit!"

And with that, the mysterious Spirit vanished into the night. Scooter climbed back into the crib and went to sleep.

First thing in the morning, there was another leapfrog game in the nursery. This time, Scooter was right in the game—bending over, jumping over everyone, laughing and shouting.

Kermit watched him in amazement.

"What happened to Scooter?" he asked Skeeter, scratching his head. "Yesterday, he didn't want to play. Today, he's having a great time."

Skeeter shrugged.

"I guess he must have been visited by the Team Spirit last night," she said.

And then she grinned.

Please Pass the Bread

One night at dinner, Baby Animal just couldn't behave himself. He reached over Baby Piggy's plate for the bread. He chewed with his mouth open. He scooped up his mashed potatoes with his fingers and stuffed them into his mouth. Nothing anyone said could make him stop.

By Randi Hacker

Illustrated by Tom Cooke

"Animal," said Baby Piggy, "stop being wild. Say 'Please pass the bread' when you want the bread."

"Animal," said Baby Kermit, "stop acting awful. Chew with your mouth closed."

"Animal," said Nanny, "please don't be so impolite. Use your fork."

But Animal didn't stop. He flicked his peas into the mashed potatoes on the other Babies' plates. Mashed potatoes and gravy splattered everywhere. A glob of potato plopped onto Nanny's nose.

"Oh, Animal," sighed Nanny. "Will you ever learn any manners?"

After dinner, Animal went to the nursery. He took all his dolls down from their shelves and sat them around the table. Then he set the table and sat down to eat with them. At first, Animal and his friends had a very good time.

"This is what I call a dinner party," said Mr. Harrison, the stuffed bear.

"Yeah," said Winslow, the windup penguin. "No one telling us what to do."

"We can behave any way we want," said Gina, the fashion-model doll.

"So let's!" said Officer Rick, the wooden policeman.

Animal looked at his dolls nervously. Why were they acting this way?

"I don't want any more of these brussels sprouts," said Mr. Harrison. He threw his brussels sprouts at Winslow.

"No one throws brussels sprouts at me and gets away with it!" said Winslow. He picked up his cup and spilled his milk right in Mr. Harrison's lap.

Mr. Harrison began to cry and scream.

Gina stood on the table with her shoes on and started posing.

"I'd rather model than eat," she said. She tossed her hair back and stepped right on Animal's plate!

Officer Rick lifted his soup bowl to his lips.

"SLUUURRRRP! SLURRRRP! AHHHHHH!" said Officer Rick, wiping his face with the back of his hand. "I just love soup!"

Animal ran back and forth from one doll to the other, but nothing he did made them stop. Things got wilder and noisier until Animal couldn't stand it anymore.

"AAAAAAAARGH!" screamed Animal.

The dolls all stared at Animal. They'd never heard him make such a sound before.

The nursery door flew open, and Nanny ran into the room.

"Are you all right, Animal?" said Nanny.

She looked around the room.

"This place is a mess," she said. "It looks as though your dolls had their own dinner party, and they behaved exactly as they wanted, didn't they?"

Animal nodded sadly.

"And it wasn't very much fun, was it?" asked Nanny.

Animal shook his head.

"And I'll bet you understand better now why manners are so important," said Nanny.

Animal nodded.

"I'll help you clean up," said Nanny.

When everything was spick and span, Nanny asked, "Would you like to come outside and play with the rest of us?"

Animal nodded and started to run through the nursery doorway. Suddenly, he skidded to a stop and motioned for Nanny to go out first. Nanny smiled, gathered Animal into her arms, and gave him a big kiss.

"Let's go out together, my polite little Animal," said Nanny.

Me and Kermit Jones

Baby Gonzo and Baby Kermit lay on their bellies on the nursery floor. They had been working on their new electric train set all day. That is, Kermit had been working. Gonzo had mostly been watching the trains go round and round and round.

By Ellen Weiss

Illustrated by Tom Cooke

"Hey, Gonzo," said Kermit, "I need your help to change the track so that it divides over here, then we can have the two locomotives going different ways, and—Gonzo, are you listening?"

"Sure, in just a minute," Gonzo mumbled. But he wasn't really listening at all. He was daydreaming about being on a real locomotive.

Kermit waited for a few minutes, but Gonzo didn't move a muscle.

"Never mind," he finally sighed. "I'll do it myself."

"Just give me another minute," Gonzo muttered. But he was far away.

In his dream, he heard the sounds of the locomotive chugging along.

"CHUG-A CHUG-A, CHUG-A CHUG-A," it went. "WHOOOOOOO!" The train whistle blasted. Gonzo turned around, and there was a frog in an engineer's cap standing beside him.

"Who are you?" Gonzo asked.

"I'm Kermit Jones, the engineer of this train," replied the frog. "And I've got to get to Kansas City on time. Will you help me throw some coal into the furnace?"

"Sure, in just a minute," Gonzo replied. "I just want to take a look around."

Gonzo walked down the length of the train. He passed big boxcars and passenger compartments. Finally he got to the caboose. For a long time, he watched as the scenery disappeared into the distance. Then he finally turned around and went back to the locomotive.

Kermit Jones had just finished shoveling the coal into the furnace when Gonzo got there. The engine picked up speed.

The train raced past houses, farms, factories, and schools. Gonzo was having a good time looking out of the window while Kermit Jones, whistling a tune, drove the train.

Suddenly, Kermit Jones slammed on the brakes. The train slowed down, screeching in protest.

"Oh, no!" said Kermit Jones. "Somebody forgot to switch the track up ahead. Gonzo," he said, "you've got to go out there and switch that track."

"Sure, in just a minute," said Gonzo. He was busy staring at a big hay wagon that was passing.

"We don't have a minute!" shouted Kermit Jones. "If you don't do it right now, we're going to run into that oncoming train!"

Gonzo looked over. Sure enough, the other train was approaching fast. There was going to be a crash! He saw the big lever he had to pull to switch the track.

He jumped out of the train and ran hard. Would he make it in time? The train smoke was in his eyes, swirling all around him.

"Now, Gonzo, now!" a voice called as the smoke cleared. He was back in the nursery, and Baby Kermit was calling to him.

Gonzo reached over and pulled the switch. The two trains whizzed harmlessly past each other.

"Whew," said Kermit. "That was close. You know, Gonzo, sometimes you can't wait to do something in just a minute—especially when someone else is relying on you."

"I see what you mean," said Gonzo. "Next time, I'll pay more attention when you ask me for help."

"Well, how about helping me now?" asked Kermit. "We need to rebuild this section of track."

"Sure!" Gonzo said. And he was busy rebuilding before anyone could say "in just a minute"!

Not Talking!

"Scooter," said Baby Skeeter one spring morning, "come and play jump-and-bump with me."

"I don't want to play jump-and-bump now," said Scooter, not looking up from his computer screen. "I want to play this computer game."

"But I want you to play with me," insisted Skeeter.

"But I'm doing something," replied Scooter. "And I don't like that game, anyhow."

By Ellen Weiss

Illustrated by Tom Cooke

"You're too boring!" said Skeeter.

"You're too bossy!" said Scooter.

"That does it," said Skeeter. "Having a twin brother is no fun. I'm going to pretend I don't even know you. I'm going to pretend I'm an only child."

"Fine," said Scooter. "I'm going to pretend I don't know you, either."

"I'm not going to play with you," said Skeeter.

"I'm not even going to talk to you," said Scooter.

"Fine," said Skeeter. "I won't talk to you, either."

And since there was no more to say, Skeeter turned away.

Petty soon, Skeeter had talked Fozzie and Animal into playing jump-and-bump with her, and they were running around the nursery like mad.

Every once in a while, Skeeter would look over at Scooter.

"Hmph," she thought to herself. "How did I ever get a brother like him, anyway? He doesn't even look like me."

Now and then, Scooter would glance up from his computer to look at Skeeter.

"She's the bossiest person in the world," he thought. "How did I ever get stuck with her, anyway?"

That afternoon, Baby Piggy had a tea party, and she invited both Scooter and Skeeter. Since they didn't want to be impolite to Piggy, they both came. But it was a little difficult.

"Piggy," said Skeeter, "would you ask Scooter to pass me a spoon, please?"

"Why don't you ask him yourself?" asked Piggy.

"I'm not talking to him," Skeeter whispered back.

They ate their bread and jam politely, in silence, for a few minutes.

"Piggy," said Scooter, "would you please tell Skeeter her napkin is on the floor?"

"This is ridiculous!" said Piggy. "Why don't you both just say you're sorry and get it over with?"

"Because," said Skeeter, "we're not talking, that's why."

Piggy sighed.

Just before dinner, Skeeter was curled up in a chair, looking at a big book and trying not to look at Scooter, whom she was actually beginning to miss.

Scooter was working at his computer, trying not to look at Skeeter.

Skeeter finished looking at the big book and climbed up to

put it back on the shelf and take out another one. The big book was heavy, though, and she didn't push it in all the way. Scooter noticed the book sticking out above Skeeter's head. If he were talking to Skeeter, of course, he'd have said, "Skeeter, you ought to push that book back." But he wasn't talking to her.

Then something happened.

Animal thumped right past Skeeter on a pogo stick, and the thumping shook the floor, and it was just enough to make the book shake loose and start to fall. And in that split second, Scooter knew that his sister was the most important person in the world to him, and if she got hurt, he'd feel just awful.

"Skeeter!" cried Scooter. "Duck!"

Luckily, Skeeter was a fast mover. She jumped up, and the book landed right where her head had been a second before.

"Thanks, Scooter!" she said. "You saved me." Then she stared. "Scooter," she said, "you're talking to me!"

"Of course I'm talking to you," said Scooter. "And you're talking to me, too. It's crazy for us not to talk to each other. You're my sister, and I love you, too, even if you are a brat sometimes."

"And I love you, too, even if you're boring sometimes," said Skeeter. "I'll never stop talking to you again."

And she didn't.

One for The Seesaw

It was a lovely, sunny fall day, and the Babies were at the playground. Baby Piggy and Baby Kermit were on the seesaw, going up and down.

Just when they were about even, Piggy looked over toward the monkey bars.

By Ellen Weiss

Illustrated by Tom Cooke

"Hey, look what Skeeter's doing," she said. "She's hanging by her knees. I want to try that."

"Don't get off yet," Kermit started saying. "I'm not ready!"

But it was too late. Piggy was already off, and Kermit hadn't had time to prepare for his landing.

Bump!

He came down hard, right on his bottom.

"Piggy, that hurt!" Kermit called, but she didn't even hear him. She was already halfway across the playground.

Kermit stood up, rubbing his sore behind. It did hurt, but that wasn't really what felt so bad. It was the surprise of hitting the ground so unexpectedly that felt bad.

Kermit went over to the sandbox. He sat down and began making a mountain. He felt nice and safe and close to the ground.

When the mountain was almost done, he heard Skeeter calling him. "Kermit!" she yelled. "Come on the seesaw!"

"No thanks, Skeeter," he called back. "I'm busy here."

In a little while, the mountain was done, but Kermit wasn't ready to leave the sandbox. He decided to make the mountain into a castle. He made some square castle-y things on top, and a road that wound around from the base to the top. Over by the seesaw, he saw Skeeter going up and down with Scooter and laughing.

Kermit decided to break up some twigs and make people to put on the road to the castle. He worked for a long time.

"Come on the seesaw with me, Kermit!" called Fozzie.

"Sorry, I'm busy," said Kermit.

Kermit was just putting a little paper flag on the very top of the castle when Piggy plunked down next to him.

"Want to try the seesaw again?" she asked.

"Not on your life," said Kermit. "You gave me a big bump last time."

"I did?" said Piggy in surprise. "I'm sorry. I guess I shouldn't have gotten off so fast. If we go back on, I promise I won't bump you. I'll be really careful."

"I don't like the seesaw," said Kermit.

"You liked the seesaw before," said Piggy. "Can't we get back on? I really won't bump you."

"No," said Kermit. "I don't want to."

"You mean you're *scared* to," said Piggy.

"Okay, I'm scared to. So I'm not going on again."

"Kermie," said Piggy, "I know it's scary to get back on, but when I fell off my tricycle, Nanny said that the best thing was to climb right back on. Please try the seesaw with me."

"Oh, all right," said Kermit.

Kermit and Piggy went over to the seesaw, and Kermit held on very tight. "Not too high," he said.

"Not too high," she agreed, and pushed off just a little bit with her toes. Pretty soon, they were going up and down, a little higher and higher still. Kermit held on tightly, but he was smiling.

"Whee!" he cried. "This is really fun!"

When it was time to go, they both got off the seesaw, very carefully.

"Thanks, Piggy," said Kermit. "I'm glad you got me back on the seesaw. I don't think I'll be scared anymore."

"I don't think so, either," said Piggy.

And she gave him a big hug.

Baby
Bunsen's
Sleep-Over
Surprise

By Jim Lewis

Illustrated by Tom Cooke

This was just about *the* most exciting day in the entire history of the nursery! You see, this was the day that Baby Bunsen and Baby Beaker were coming for a sleep-over with the Babies! They were going to stay all night, laughing, singing, playing games—maybe even sleeping. Best of all, they had promised to bring a big surprise!

"They're coming!" shouted Baby Gonzo, who was watching at the nursery window. "And they have the surprise with them!"

"I bet Bunsen has invented a banana-powered joke machine," said Baby Fozzie.

"I think it's a supercharged piano," called Baby Rowlf.

"It's probably an out-of-this world adventure maker so I can have even more adventures," insisted Baby Piggy. "I'm quite adventurous, you know."

"Sheesh! It doesn't matter if they bring us any surprise," said Baby Kermit. "The real fun is that Bunsen and Beaker are coming for a sleep-over."

At last, the door to the nursery opened. It was Nanny with Baby Bunsen and Baby Beaker! The sleep-over had begun, and everyone let out a great big "Yaaay!"

"What a great pleasure to be here," said Bunsen. Beaker squeaked in agreement.

But before Bunsen and Beaker could put down their sleep-over knapsacks, Fozzie asked, "Is the surprise a banana-powered joke machine?"

"Is it a supercharged piano?" asked Rowlf.

"Is it an out-of-this-world adventure maker so I can have more adventures?" asked Piggy.

"Sheesh!" said Kermit. "I'm sure Bunsen and Beaker will tell us when they're ready."

"There's no need to wait," said Bunsen. "Beaker and I have brought you an all-new invention that will change sleep-overs forever—the sneaky sleepy snoozing machine." And with that, Beaker took out a very strange-looking invention. It was covered with lights and buzzers, knobs and dials, and made a sound like this: "ZZZZZZZZZZZZ!"

"Your machine is snoring," said Piggy.

"I think it's asleep," said Rowlf.

"Precisely," said Bunsen. "The sneaky sleepy snoozing machine sleeps for you. That means we can stay up all night, laughing, singing, playing games—and we won't have to sleep even a little."

"So I can stay up all night telling jokes?" said Fozzie.

"And I can play my piano 'til sunrise?" asked Rowlf.

"And I can have adventures all night long?" said Piggy.

Everyone was *very* excited.

But Kermit was not excited, not excited at all.

"No, thank you," he said to Bunsen and Beaker. "That sounds like fun, but I'd miss sleeping."

"You would?" asked the Babies.

"Sure," said Kermit. "I'd miss my warm, cuddly blankets, my big soft pillow, and, most of all, I'd miss my dreams."

"Hmm," said Bunsen. "I guess we didn't think of that. Those are all quite lovely—especially the dreams."

"When I'm dreaming, I have some very exciting adventures," explained Piggy.

Everyone else nodded in agreement.

So Baby Bunsen, Baby Beaker, and the other Babies put away the sneaky sleepy snoozing machine. They told jokes, sang songs, played games, and had lots of sleep-over fun.

And when bedtime came, they went to sleep in their warm, cuddly, big soft beds.

Because, after all, what fun is a sleep-over without sleeping . . . and dreaming?

THE END